About the author

A well travelled New Zealander and self professed sports fan, Tony now lives in Berkshire in the United Kingdom with two of his four children, the other two having now flown the nest. He has carried a love of writing for many years.

Semaine was born and nurtured in different cafés in Asia, the Pacific, North America and Europe. Tony has had a passion for personal development and in addition to Semaine, has two other books percolating in the atmosphere of different cafés.

Tony's vision is to provide a different perspective to those living on our planet. To acknowledge the importance of family, to embrace change, to strive to be our best every day, to accept the art of the "possible" (man has walked on the moon after all); and to encourage each individual to make a difference to our world.

Semaine

A story for our time…

A story by

Tony Henderson-Newport

Story illustrations by

Amanda Stiler

Book Cover illustrations and design by

Charmian Eamus and Gemma Laidlaw

This book is a work of fiction. Names, characters, places and incidents are either the product of the author's imagination or are used fictitiously, and any resemblance to actual persons living or dead, businesses, companies, events or locales is entirely coincidental.

ISBN 978-0-9555491-1-3

British Library Cataloguing in Publication Data.

A catalogue record for this book is available from the British Library.

Copyright Registration Number: 60800035

Dedication

This book is dedicated to Mavis and Leit

They blessed me with their love and proved to me what parenting was all about… even if it did take me more than a few years to figure out even a fraction of what they knew.

Thanks

A project like this can only become real when people pitch in and provide the most amazing support. Over the years of Semaine's coming of age, there were so many people who listened, read, provided positive and constructive feedback that enabled Semaine to become more real with each comment.

I would like to mention some people who held the baby along the way: Debbie Hipperson, Bob and Sarah Seath, Bill Fuller, Loren Martin, Alex Greig and their daughter Gwenyth, Elaine Turner, Megan Bone. Amanda Stiler who did all the story illustrations in the book, Megan Kerr my amazing editor and proof reader, the multi-talented Gemma Laidlaw who amongst other things can do incredible things with image design, Charmian Eamus who can draw the socks off you, Adrian Cubitt whose talent is all about video, Bryony Hampton, our wonderful media consultant and pseudo kiwi, Tess Hood my Audio advisor and Max Hunt the producer. Francine and Teo Hodge, and Francisca de Juan who kept our feet planted in Spanish culture; and of course my amazing friend and buddy, Phil Gladwell who provided all of the technology needs. Phil has gone above and beyond over many years, putting up with his zany friend.

A huge thank you goes to the Living Rainforest in Berkshire, UK. They enabled the creative team to see chameleons in action. This experience still resonates in a positive way. For more information please go to: www.livingrainforest.org.

Thanks must also go to the myriad of entrepreneurs around the world who have kept me inspired over the years. Keeping a dream alive is a critical part of making it real. Thanks also to the numerous Costa cafés around the UK and Europe who have put up with the guy in the corner obviously trying to figure things out over a Flat White!

Of course this thank you wouldn't be complete with out a mention to my children here in the United Kingdom and in New Zealand, whom I just love to bits. I can just hear their, “uh oh, Dad's off again!” or… “come on Dad, not Costa again!” They inspire me every day to create a different future.

Authors Note

There is something about creation. We have an amazing planet. We humans are unique and yet… so are the myriad of bird, sea, insect and wildlife that co-habit with us.

Choosing a chameleon was deliberate. They have several characteristics that make them unique. An amazing ability to change their kaleidoscopic skin. Then, they have independently rotating eyes. This is incredible from two aspects. Firstly, imagine the perspective through which chameleons view their world. Then there is the laser like focus that occurs when a chameleon is about to snare its prey, because what happens next is incredible… Watching a slow motion view of a chameleon catching its prey with its tongue makes you understand "blink and you have missed it" in a whole new way.

Chameleon colonies speak to me of family, and then there is the way chameleons co-exist with other native species in the wild.

This leads me nicely onto the whole element of the spirituality and connectedness of nature, always finding ways to be its best. The way nature adapts and enables re-growth and regeneration is at the core of evolution. It is this willingness, sometimes by necessity, to adapt, to change that is at the heart of this story. Change is continual and yet for nature it is something that always contains a new future. For millennia we have seen the gradual and continual evolution of our planet and its inhabitants.

We have also seen the impact of an ever growing human civilisation on our planet, its habitats and now, sadly, many species have been assigned a tagline: extinct!

This is a story then about the importance of change and how we can deal with it. It is about family and unexpected friendships. It is about the underlying spirituality that I believe exists in our world.

Semaine then is a chance to view events from a different perspective; that of a young chameleon on an amazing adventure.

Semaine

A story for our time…

Prologue

Semaine was confused. He wasn't prepared for this. He'd intended to have an adventure, but now he felt trapped, confined, bewildered, anxious, afraid… he wasn't used to feeling afraid. Or at least, not this kind of fear.

In his world, survival was a daily event. In his world, life and death were as natural as rubbing against a branch. In his world, fear was an inherent part of his instincts for survival.

This fear, however, was primal. His whole being was affected by the loss of his senses. He could not see, touch, hear, or feel. The blackness, the silence, was overpowering. His normal, considered movements had fled—he was frozen. And yet, he could think. He could sense. Perhaps irrationally, this made him even more afraid. *What ifs?* surfaced quickly, redoubling his fear.

What if I'm lost forever? What if I never see my family again? What if I can't get back? And another question raised its head, too. *Am I dead?*

It had been a risk. But that's what all good adventures were, a risk. But this—this wasn't fair. Why couldn't he have a story to tell, just like the other times he'd returned to the colony? It was not fair.

Bleak, black thoughts were new to Semaine. In fact, he was so used to coping with anything that this new situation had immobilised his instincts and his mind. He simply could not think coherently. He'd heard from others of his species about times they'd been afraid, and he had secretly thought how he would have handled the same situation. Now, he was just plain scared. It was a bitter truth for him to face: he was, quite simply, scared to death.

Chapter 1

On a warm summer's day, all those years ago, the peace of the forest was shattered by the laughter and sounds of children crashing through the undergrowth.

Semaine was drifting in the memories of a lesson his father had patiently explained.

"Now Semaine, focus clearly on the beauty in the shape and you will find your form easily and naturally."

He'd practised and practised. Every now and then, he knew he was more than just good. His defence mechanism was unusual. His senses were highly attuned to recognise danger, allowing him precious extra seconds—seconds that could allow him to live another day. His parents had instilled the need to practise continually. His surroundings became his classroom. Nature, the most voracious of teachers, also graciously provided the lessons to learn. And so, like his ancestors before him, he practised the art and science of survival.

He found that he loved the challenge of learning; of how close he could be to those who would take his life, for his classroom was also their playground. He didn't take risks—he just needed to understand how far he could develop his skill, and it was this drive for understanding that challenged him.

CRASH! BANG!

Semaine tensed, perched on the old stump in the sunny corner of the leafy glade.

Creatures he'd never seen before burst into the sunshine, four of them. Three walked on two legs with big humps on their backs while the fourth ran on four legs and made strange, loud noises. The others emitted quick chattering sounds, as if they were communicating with each other.

The group of three waited at the edge of the clearing while Semaine watched. They turned to each other, pointing at his spot. Then as a group, they moved towards him. He froze. Some deeply ingrained instinct focused him and compelled him to be still. He could feel the grain, texture, and colours of the stump. He could almost feel it breathe as he slipped into the world of alternate reality. Was he really there?

The group stopped below his vantage point and started taking the humps off their backs. They made a strange shape from the contents, like a shelter they could hide in, of a colour he'd never seen before. When they went into the shelter, he couldn't see them.

As he watched, Semaine's mind raced. Who were they? *What* were they?

The afternoon sun moved on and as it began to set, the creatures leapt into action. Next to the coloured shelter, they created a flickering light. Over this light, the visitors placed other objects and strange new aromas permeated the atmosphere.

Semaine was intrigued and as dark descended, he carefully crept down to where the strangers sat around the flickering light, making sure he stayed in the shadows.

Only the strangers' intermittent chirruping broke the stillness of the evening. For a short while, their voices took on a new dimension as they worked in unison, rising and falling, creating a pleasant sound—something like birdsong, but deeper, slower, and less skilful. Slowly the flickering light dimmed. He edged closer, his curiosity overcoming his fear of discovery. On the fringe of their circle, he stiffened as the group all moved at once. He watched, quiet and alert, as they moved into the coloured shelter. When at last they were still, he resumed his quest, his exploration of something new and different. Gentle reminders came to him in his father's voice, cautioning him to always be careful, reminding him that his strength lay in his apparent invisibility. Instinctively, Semaine knew that the four-legged creature presented his biggest risk of discovery. At that moment, his adventure in full flight, he had no idea he was about to change his life forever.

He reached the coloured shelter. He stretched out and touched the surface—smooth yet complex, a myriad of uniform patterns. It was unlike anything he had encountered previously. It was strange, almost as if it had no life force. It didn't breathe like the trees and plants he lived with. Instinctively cautious, he edged into the shelter. It was quiet and dark. The only sound was the gentle breathing of the strange beings, wrapped in colourful cocoons on the floor of the shelter.

One of their hands was resting lightly on the ground near Semaine. He studied its complexion and texture. He stretched out his tongue and gently touched the skin. It was soft and warm. He felt light hairs on the skin and sensed the gentle pulse of the being's life force. Withdrawing his tongue, he moved closer. He touched the hand. As he did so, sensations flooded his mind. He drew back quickly, breathing hard.

What had happened? It was as if he had new perceptions and feelings, confusing visions and sensations. He kept still, collecting his thoughts. Summoning up his courage, he again stretched out and touched the hand. This time, he was ready for the changes and thoughts that flooded his mind. Remaining as detached as he could from the strange sensations, he stepped slowly forward onto the hand. The sensations almost overwhelmed him. He was sensing texture, warmth, peacefulness, but at the same time part of him trembled with tension, like a drop of water about to fall from a leaf.

He now stood almost completely on the being's hand. Gently, he stretched out further, relinquishing the floor of the strange cave to balance on the being's skin. He now allowed himself to gently explore this unusual surface, this living organism. A strange picture rushed in his mind… a large gleaming object, belching bad-smelling mist from its rear, was hurtling along two straight shiny sticks that disappeared into the distance. Then he stood by a large lake, which reflected the rays of the calm, serene moon.

How can I see these things? He thought.

Suddenly, it happened. The four-legged creature pushed its head through the shelter's opening and started sniffing in Semaine's direction. Instinct took over: Semaine froze in fright, then focused on what he needed to do. He remembered his father's lessons. He thought of all the hours he had practised. And he focused. He felt his own rhythm becoming attuned to the hand and forearm on which he was lightly resting. He felt its colour, its warmth. He sensed the being's life force as he sought to find the harmony between himself and it.

The four-legged creature trotted into the tent, approaching Semaine. Semaine knew that his presence had been sensed, but not recognised. He forced himself to forget the creature and relaxed again into the sensations that heightened his awareness.

Again, his mind flooded with pictures. His heart slowed as he found the pulse of the creature's life force and matched his own life force to its. Texture, light, life, love—Semaine's vision, his very being was filled with deep love and warmth. He saw an explosion of reds and whites, shapes he'd never experienced before, as he blended totally with the being.

Flushed with success and achievement, he knew that the animal searching for him could no longer see or sense him. Exhausted, he relaxed, certain he could hold the change. He slipped into tired unconsciousness, still aware that his transition was deep, and different from anything he'd previously experienced.

And then he slept.

Chapter 2

It was a voice of peace—warm, deep and relaxing. Semaine knew he could trust it, for he'd heard it before. Waking from his sleep, Semaine kept still, listening, conscious that something about his surroundings had changed.

"When we stretch to new horizons," it said, *"we find new lands—lands of peace and harmony, lands still requiring courage, resolve, and love."*

Whenever the voice spoke to him, it always carried a message that he could learn from. He knew that it was always there to support him. It provided direction in times of crisis, and harmony in times of peace. The key, Semaine had learnt, was to really listen to the voice. The challenge from the voice's message was perhaps to act differently to how he had in the past, to change subtly or dramatically to ensure the desired result. Semaine knew the voice was acknowledging him for having stretched and also telling him that he would still need courage and love as he continued his journey.

What's different? he wondered. His slow awakening and reflections couldn't calm his growing disquiet.

In the stillness before dawn, when the dark still lingers, Semaine's consciousness was noticing a difference. A different blackness. A different silence. A different feel to his surroundings. A difference he realised he could not actually feel—a difference that seemed to exist all around him. He was becoming anxious. Where was he? He stretched his thoughts out. Nothing.

Nothing! How can there be nothing?

He reached back in his mind, reviewing his last memories. It rushed back: his adventure. Foolhardy, stupid even, and yet it had been his adventure. But what had happened? He had crept onto the hand of the stranger, then the four-legged creature had entered the shelter and he had blended and escaped… or had he?

Fear wasn't new to Semaine. You couldn't live in the forest and not experience fear. Fear in his environment was manageable because it was known. This fear was different. The type that comes from the unexplained. Now, however, fear, real fear, was distracting his ability to think. He had never felt more alone and for perhaps the first time his thoughts were very bleak indeed.

And then the strangest thing happened.

He felt his eyes opening and slowly focusing. Something was different about his vision, but what? The colours of the shelter floated above him. The cocoon that he and the being had lain in still enfolded him. The sun filtered though the shelter's roof. Another voice clamoured—a young voice—and he recognised the sounds from the night before.

The view changed towards the two cocoons on the floor. The other beings were still asleep. Semaine was rooted to the spot, the fear so tangible that he could taste it.

What's happening? he thought, feeling ill and disoriented.

Abruptly, the view changed again. This time, he sensed that the being was going to leave its cocoon. Semaine desperately wanted somewhere to hide, his anxiety reaching new levels. Why had he slept so long? Surely he would be discovered—and then what? Oh, why had he wanted to explore the shelter and the new sights so much? And why was he seeing things so strangely? He was used to seeing different objects at the same time, in different directions, his eyes rotating independently. Now he was seeing straight ahead, the most unusual perspective imaginable, and more frightening still was that he had no control over what he was seeing. How could this be? What was more, he couldn't move—but all his instincts told him he wasn't paralysed or frozen. He also knew he was holding the best blend he had ever achieved.

His view shifted to outside the shelter, a beautiful sunny morning. The trees shone green and the faintest of breezes stirred the leaves into the day. Only when a hand reached out into his view to stir the embers of last night's fire did Semaine realise the truth of his situation: he was inside the being.

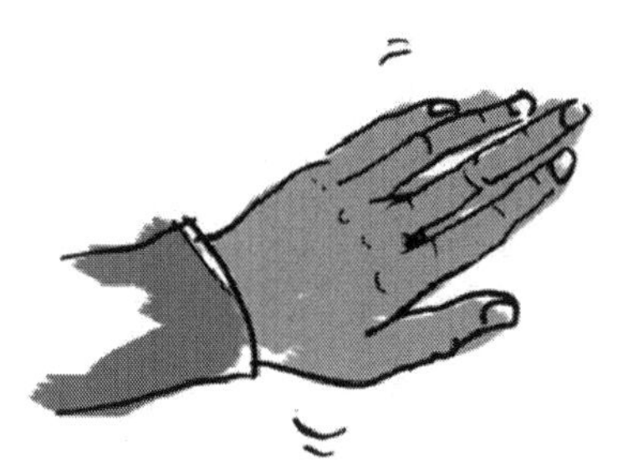

Chapter 3

Deep-rooted fear gripped him as he saw the enormity of his predicament. Just before, in the quiet dark, he had experienced a fear he had not experienced before. Now he was quite simply scared to death. He desperately sought to escape. But how? His mind seemed frozen; he felt lost and unprepared. He knew, too, that now he could draw on all his hours and hours of practising to be the best he could be. To choose his responses was, he knew, essential. Now, his courage and his adventurous spirit were being challenged. Now, he must choose to become calm. CALM. Calm was the last thing he felt. His thoughts raced but didn't seem to go anywhere. He felt stuck. Calm – but how? His father used to say that his best decisions came when he was calm. Right; easy for him to say! His mind flashed on his father again. "Come on Semaine!" he could hear his father saying, "concentrate." As he concentrated he began, ever so slightly, to calm. His breathing and his thoughts seemed to slow just a little and in the tiny space between his panic attacks he remembered the voice and its message: *"When we stretch, we see new horizons. We find new lands, lands of peace and harmony, lands still requiring courage, resolve, and love."*

Messages within circles, thought Semaine. Even in crisis, he reflected, focusing on the message brought its own peace—and, possibly, the solutions he sought. Again, he tried to slow his racing thoughts, and mentally probed his surroundings.

If I have blended into this creature, maybe I can blend out again.

His whole being was alert as he absorbed the sensations around him. He heard the being rustling through the bush. He felt the warmth of the sun and detected a gentle murmuring in the background, almost constant, only so low as to be almost unnoticeable. Only because of his heightened alertness had Semaine caught it. Now, he mentally searched for it, probing with his mind, wondering if this were the key to his escape.

The sound was more of a gentle 'buzz' of noise; like insects gathering around rotten food. It was noticeable mainly because he was in so much silence. Every now and then something seemed familiar in the 'noise'. He strung the familiar "sounds" together and started to hear a pattern. It was familiar but different, a string of symbols and expressions that he abruptly recognised were thoughts. Thoughts that were in the language of this being! Was this the key? Understand the thoughts, interpret the meanings, and work out the possibilities to communicate and escape.

Semaine concentrated on the thoughts. They were light, like a new spring morning; relaxed, like the soft spring breeze; and refreshing, like the crisp clean air after a spring shower. He sensed feelings and emotions, too—again similar to his own but different. The being was starting to feel hungry. And because this being felt warm, Semaine was also feeling warm. Semaine's inherent curiosity, his love of exploring puzzles, was, for the moment keeping him calm. His predicament though was real and had not gone away. Slowly Semaine let his thoughts change direction and ever so slightly he allowed his mind to explore his surroundings and these strange new sounds.

How do I understand? he thought, perplexed. *How do our thoughts reach out and touch each other so we can understand? Can this being also sense that something is different?*

Little did he realise how these questions would be answered, or the adventures that would befall him as he was carried on in a quest that had now taken on a life of its own.

When she awoke, Maria felt disoriented. Cocooned in her sleeping bag she felt cosy and yet... not! Maria was not a creature of habit, although the quiet time before getting out of bed had always captivated her. She had that impetuous and bold approach that typified the pre teen and teen generations of all ages. Music was also something that captured her thoughts. It had always been that way. Since she was a baby listening to her mother singing her goodnight or her father humming to the sounds on the radio. When the people in her town got together, she loved the harmonies and melodies they created, mixing instrument and voice. She wondered about the mysterious element woven into the harmonies, which brought people together. It was as if the music danced with her mind, in harmony with the others. The campfire last night and the singing with her papá and brother were special moments for her.

Maria heaved a deep satisfied sigh as she waited for her father and brother Ramón to wake into the day. And yet she felt restless and was not sure why. She knew that tonight they would be home, sharing a family meal as they unfolded the story of the adventurous weekend trek to their mother. She loved it when her mother came camping. This time she had been drawn away at the last minute by a sick cousin in another village.

Her thoughts were chaotic, flitting from one thought to the next, settling for brief moments and then off again. She thought of the campfire songs from the night before and the strange dreams she'd had. She wondered why they had been so clear. She'd dreamed before, but these dreams seemed almost real— and she felt so strange. When she first woke up, she'd felt disoriented with a feeling she couldn't quite place. It was like the time she'd climbed a tree, then found she couldn't get down and had been rescued by her father. She rose and sat quietly by the colourful tent her mother had carefully stitched for them when her father took them trekking in the wilderness. It was strange, she thought, strange to feel something was not quite the same and not to know why.

The dog, Vito, watched her quizzically as if he also knew something was different.

Her father's cheerful "Good morning!" interrupted Maria's thoughts. How she loved this time with her father before her brother Ramón woke up.

Her father started a small fire and was soon making breakfast. Tantalising aromas wafted into the fresh morning air, reminding her how hungry she was. A hearty breakfast was essential before they started their trek back to the Jeep.

Like a ball fired from a cannon, Ramón exploded into the day. He was two years younger than Maria and carried the energy of a youngster alive with life and adventure. Maria was both wary of Ramón's excitable zest and when they 'got on' enjoyed his excitable nature. They 'got on' okay most of the time, but Maria was turning into a teen and was now very intolerant of Ramón's pranks and schoolboy jokes. Now he fell into the 'pain' category.

Her life would soon change, she reflected, and these memories would be important for her. She was in her last year at primary school and was due to leave for secondary school in a nearby town after this school year. Her new school was one her parents had saved hard for her to attend. It would be a big change for her. The longer daily commute by bus would be a lot different from the gentle walk to school she currently experienced.

Her father and Ramón were chatting away as Maria finished her breakfast. It wasn't that she felt sick, rather it was like being slightly off centre and not being able to correct it. She also noticed, strangely, that the breakfast and forest smells seemed stronger, more real... although she thought... that doesn't make sense! Before long, the campfire was put out, the tent packed, and with a last look to ensure the camp site was returned gratefully to nature, they started their journey home.

Semaine was puzzled. He now knew where he was and his instincts were flying fast, looking for openings to escape—but he also knew somehow he was safe, and could explore without panic.

He'd got closer to the sounds drifting on in the background. Those sounds, he was sure, were the key to it all. He allowed his mind to embrace them. They were disjointed, sometimes running together, sometimes random. What was the connection, if there was one? They seemed cheerful, questioning, thoughtful, unsure and happy, by turns. Was that it? What if he matched the feelings and emotions expressed by the sounds? They had quietened while he was thinking this. His view was of a beautiful forest, branches whipping past his vision. He'd never felt speed before and it left him fascinated, intrigued, and a little disorientated.

The sound began once more, and this time he embraced the emotions and feelings surrounding it. He experienced relaxation, exertion, wonder and anticipation. He let himself absorb the feelings fully and as he did so, he recognised a sound: "HILL". It startled him so much that the sound went back to its monotone. Semaine was still. His instincts had frozen him back into his natural behaviour when the unexpected had happened.

He knew that he had made a breakthrough. "Hill!" He had heard it clearly and strongly. Relaxing himself, he started to absorb the sound and embrace the emotions again. As he settled back into the sound he heard, "Wow, almost at the top of the hill, then not far to the Jeep."

The voice was high-pitched but calm, animated and interested—a young voice, sensed Semaine, and happy.

As they reached the top of the hill, the view spread into a panorama of blue sky, forested hills and a blue ocean stretching to the horizon. It was a stunning display of the earth's beauty and affected Semaine deeply. Without thinking, he said, "Wow, look at that!"

Maria reached the rise and paused as the view unfolded before her. As she drank in the scene's beauty, she heard someone say, "Wow, look at that!" She knew it wasn't her father or brother's voice. She glanced left, right, behind her—nothing.

"Who said that?" she asked.

Her father and brother looked at her, startled. They'd all stopped to take in the view, dropping their packs on the ground.

"Did you hear someone say something, Papá?" asked Maria.

"No. Maybe it was Ramón's pack, hitting the ground."

"Maybe," said Maria, unconvinced.

Semaine again embraced the sounds and emotions.

"I know I heard a voice," the sounds said.

Semaine remained quiet.

"This is strange, why can't I see anyone?"

He sensed that the voice was feminine, like his mother, but much younger. He felt he could trust this person, but he was worried: each moment took him further from his beloved glade, further from his home and from his family.

"My name is Semaine, please don't be scared," he said quickly, almost before he could think what to say.

Maria stood still. Quiet. She glanced around her. Nothing. No one was in sight, apart from Ramón and her father sitting quietly, leaning against a tree after their hike up from the valley floor.

"Did you hear anything, Ramón?" she asked.

"No, Maria, nothing. It's so quiet."

She went still again. The voice had been quiet and firm, reassuring. It had said it was called Semaine. It had said not to be scared—she sensed it was right.

Where are you hiding? she thought. *I know I heard someone speak.*

Semaine held quiet a moment, aware he'd made contact.

"My name is Semaine," he said softly. "I don't know how I got here and I need your help."

She listened attentively to the voice—gentle, concerned, and, she thought, disquieted. She scanned the hillside yet again for some sight of its owner, to no avail.

The voice was so close.

"I'm inside you," said Semaine. "It's our thoughts that are talking."

She knew immediately this was true. "But how? And why haven't you spoken before?"

"Because this only happened last night and I want to see my home and family again," said Semaine.

"But how?" Maria asked again. Agitation mixed with extreme curiosity.

Semaine sensed that he needed to slow down. He took a deep breath and said quietly, "If I tell you, will you help me to get home?"

Her father rose and came over to her.

"Are you all right, Maria? You're unusually quiet," he said as he put his arm around her and hugged her close.

"Yes, papá." she said. "Papá, do you ever hear voices?"

"You mean like in my mind?"

"Yes," she said. "What does it mean?"

Her father was silent for a moment. "Maria, we all have a voice inside us, a voice that can guide us. A voice that can give us answers to our dreams, challenges we never dreamt of and paths to follow. Have you been hearing a voice?" he asked gently.

"Yes, Papá." she said.

"Well, Maria," said her father, "listen carefully to the voice and act well. Remember what your mama and I have brought you and Ramón up to believe in. The voice will guide you. If you doubt its intentions, or it feels wrong, then ask me or your mama for our help."

"I will," she said.

"Good. Now we must go if we want to be back home for dinner, your mama will be waiting." He picked up her pack and helped her to put it on her back.

Ramón was already bouncing up and down, eager to march on towards the Jeep. The dog, Vito, was quietly watching Maria.

As they resumed walking, Maria thought quietly, "Are you still there Semaine?"

"Hello Maria," he said. "Yes, I'm still here." He'd been quiet, listening carefully, aware for the first time that he could understand the conversation between Maria and her father. Semaine reflected on the similarities between their fathers: gentle guidance and support were at the core of Maria's father's comments and of his own father's advice.

"Are you the voice my Papá was talking about?" asked Maria.

Semaine thought carefully and said, "Maria, what your Papá said was true for me, too. I have this little voice that talks to me. Only I don't have conversations with it like you and I are having now. When my voice speaks in those still quiet moments, and I really listen, it guides me."

"Are you that voice for me?" she asked.

"No, Maria. I'm Semaine. Last night, I went on an adventure to see one of your kind and I ended up here. Maria, I am a chameleon—a colour-changer, who blends with nature and loves being in harmony with the beauty of life. Last night, in my quest for adventure, I crept onto your wrist while you slept. In a moment of fright, I blended, as is the way of my kind, and I blended into you. And now," he said in a shaky voice, "I don't know how to get out and I know that with every step I'm moving further away from my home and my family."

He fell silent. Maria's mind reeled with the words that he'd spoken. Semaine sensed her confusion and knew he could do nothing now except wait. He knew also that it was important for him to tell the truth and not hide anything from Maria.

The forest was refreshing and entrancing. The rich blue sky enhanced the canopy of the teeming forest. Semaine and Maria were both lost in their own uncertain dream. Both were experiencing the uncertainty of the unknown. Neither could see a clear solution. The two were bonded by an unusual event, something private and significant which would forever change their lives.

After a while, Maria spoke, soft and cautious. "I'm frightened," she said. "I don't know what to think or what to do."

Semaine remained silent, not wishing to interrupt her thoughts but also wanting to support her. He thought of his mother and how when he'd been troubled or confused, she was always there with a gentle, reassuring touch, and a wise word of guidance.

As if echoing his thoughts, Maria thought, *Maybe if I speak with papá or mama, they can help.* She also thought, *Will they believe me?*

The terrain was opening out as they reached the edge of the forest where the Jeep was parked. Time had been passing as they explored their thoughts.

"Are you there, Semaine?" asked Maria.

"Yes," he answered, cautiously and quietly.

"Since we are together, so to speak, why don't we find out about each other by asking each other questions? Do you think that would be all right?"

Semaine agreed and for the next little while they traded ages, families, and adventures. Semaine talked about the forest he loved so much.

"You know," said Maria, "this is not just a forest. It's a Rainforest. That means that because of where we are on the earth the temperature and the plants and trees are different from other forests. Rainforest's also have animals and insects that you will not find in forests."

Semaine was intrigued by the new information because he had not mixed with other species or beings before. Certainly he had not been out of his, what did Maria call it, his rainforest. Then something else occurred to Semaine.

"What do you mean by where we live on the earth?"

"Well," said Maria, "We live in a small town called Zalamea la Real. It is near a very large town called Huelva which is near two even bigger towns, which are called Sevilla and Cadiz. In our country, called Spain, we have a number of large areas of land which are called regions. Our region is called Andalucía. I learned about this at school. Because we are closer to the middle of the earth, the temperatures are higher and the air is often more humid. That means that there is often more water in the air than normal and often more rain. And that is why it is called a rainforest. So it is the climate that makes it like a rainforest. Also, I learned that Andalucía has more areas to protect our wildlife than anywhere else in Spain."

Semaine was quiet for a moment and then he said, his voice shaking slightly, "It might have a different name but it's my home and with every step you take, I get further away from my home and my family. I don't like it Maria. I don't like this at all."

"You know, Semaine, we can always come back here when we figure all this out." Maria's voice, expressed her concern for her new friend.

Soon they reached the top of the hill and ventured a little way into the trees where Semaine encountered yet another strange being. In fact this one seemed very still and was a little shiny where the sunshine crept through the leafy canopy to bounce off the skin of the enormous creature. Maria explained that it was their method of transport. They were at an old, covered Jeep that Maria's father and mother had bought for trips into the countryside.

This was all new to Semaine. Even the walk had amazed him as the scenery whisked past at blinding speed. He was still getting used to Maria's shape, her being. Then there were her relationships with her brother and father, and now this strange-shaped being into which they were throwing their packs and sleeping bags.

Semaine had no time to reflect the new being's strangeness as Maria opened up the side of the being and climbed inside. 'Overwhelmed' would not describe Semaine's emotions and feelings because he was literally in sensory overload. Each second brought fresh concepts to think about. Because of this his senses were dulled but not dead. Just numb. Semaine could still see outside, thanks to a large opening in front of him, but that opening also looked different—as if he could see outside the being, but through something else.

He watched as Maria's father stopped what he was doing and looked at the distant sky. Black clouds were gathering in the distance. Reaching into his pocket he pulled out a small strange shaped object and started punching it with his finger before putting it up to his ear. He then spoke into the thing. His voice was anxious,

"Carlos, I don't like what I can see out to sea. I think a real bad storm is on its way". Enrique listened for a few minutes and then after saying goodbye pressed the little black box and put it in his pocket.

"I don't like it." he said when he had got back into the Jeep. "Carlos said that Hurricane warnings were out for southern coastal Spain."

Maria quickly explained about mobile phones and hurricanes.

"Maria, I don't know much about what you have told me... but I do know there is a really big storm coming. I can sense it."

The openings on the Jeep closed with strange noises, then Maria's father started fiddling around. Semaine jumped, thrown into confusion, as the being's roar reverberated through the forest. The new being became a beast as it shook and spluttered into life. Maria immediately sensed his fright and acted quickly to calm him.

"It's okay, Semaine," she thought. "It's just the sound of the Jeep. It's how we travel from place to place instead of walking."

But it was too late. Semaine was badly shaken. He'd never heard anything like this in his life before. The noise deafened him. He realised that he'd almost lost contact with Maria in his fright. If she hadn't spoken to him when she did, he knew he would have attempted to blend.

He realised then that he didn't know what he would blend with. He wasn't in his normal environment. He wasn't on a leaf or a branch. Instead, he was feeling sensations through Maria's body rather than his own. Maria had said that she too was experiencing greater perceptions of colour and touch. His thoughts were interrupted again as he took in his surroundings and got another fright. In this strange *Jeep*, while he had been reflecting, Maria's father had started driving them home. He had thought things were moving fast before, they now seemed to be travelling at the speed of light.

Maria was sitting in the front seat beside her father. Looking out through her eyes to the path ahead, Semaine—who travelled only slowly and sometimes stayed in the same position for hours—felt his mind expand. The world and time rushed towards him at breakneck speed, a blur of colour and sound. He watched, stunned, as trees and bushes leapt past the Jeep.

He realised that he was being dragged away from his home. He felt powerless and alone. His predicament was gut wrenching. He screamed for help, but his screams were buried inside Maria and drowned in madness as he was swept along on a journey that was now out of his control.

Chapter 4

Semaine was in many ways saved by Maria who unwittingly gave Semaine something else to focus on.

"*Semaine, Semaine…*" he heard the words but for a little while they just didn't register. It was the increasing tone of Maria's voice that finally made an impact.

"What did you say?" He asked Maria.

"Semaine, thank goodness, I thought you had disappeared?" she said.

"I was here, just in shock of everything," said Semaine, "and the speed; everything seems fast and chaotic. I'm amazed at the speed we're moving, without any effort."

"Oh, this is slow compared to the motorways," she answered. "On the motorway it's a lot smoother and we go a lot faster."

"What are motorways?"

Maria explained about roads and how they connected towns and cities. She explained about cars and planes and boats. Semaine listened attentively; realising for the first time how much existed outside his beloved forest. She explained about people, families, and cultures. She talked about how humans lived in houses and wore clothes to keep warm. Semaine was again in information overload.

Time flew by as the enormity of his position became clear to him. He was in a strange body, with new emotions and experiences, and a strange world with new customs and relationships. He lapsed into silence, feeling alone and apprehensive.

In this silence, the voice spoke to him again, in gentle strength and peacefulness. *"Semaine, remember that your darkest moments are the seeds of your greatest growth. Listen to your heart and follow your spirit as it journeys on."* Semaine listened attentively as the voice continued, *"Courage will be your strength, and love will be your friend."*

This time Semaine's response was more petulant. *For goodness sake,* he thought, *please give me a solution?* In the silence that followed, Semaine struggled to put aside his frustration as he grasped for a meaning in yet another riddle. He recognised that there were some important words to hold onto: heart, spirit, courage, love, friend, and journey. It seemed small solace, but in his loneliness he was desperate for guidance and hope. Once again, the mysterious voice had delivered something, small maybe, but something. His frustration though was still evident as he mentally moved the words around in his mind.

What the voice said was true. He *was* on a journey. He *did* already have one friend. He remembered his family with love, and as he did so he felt his spirit lift. His courage and resolve became part of his consciousness. Calmer and less tense, he relaxed into a deep untroubled sleep, oblivious, for the moment, to the events that would unfold in this world of humans in which he had become an unexpected participant.

Maria sensed that Semaine was asleep. His absence from her feelings was different than when they had first entered the Jeep. Now the absence was more natural. She was stunned by the events that had unfolded and up until now she had managed to keep her promise to Semaine. But she knew she had to trust someone with her secret, but who? Minutes later her father pulled into a service station to get fuel for the Jeep and it was then that Maria decided to confide in her brother.

"Ramón," she said, "Can you keep a secret?"

"Of course I can." responded Ramón. It was not often that Maria shared secrets so Ramón was very curious about what Maria had to say.

"Well, I have a big secret. I have a being living inside of me." said Maria.

“Yeah right, pull the other one Maria. I thought you really had a secret.”

“I do, I do.” implored Maria. “Listen, you know how quiet I have been since the campsite.” Ramón nodded his head. “Well, I have a chameleon inside of me. I don’t know how but I do know it talks to me. Please believe me Ramón.”

“Your imagination has gone haywire Maria. You want *me* to believe you have a chameleon in *your* tummy. You must think I am a real idiot brother or something.”

“It’s true, its true Ramón you’ve got you’ve got to listen to me.”

Ramón pulled a face that said *liar, liar* but said nothing.

“Oh I hate you Ramón. You’re the worst brother ever. And to think I thought about sharing secrets with you.”

Just then their father got back into the Jeep catching the last part of Maria’s comments.

“Listen you two,” he said, “we’ve have had a pretty good weekend so far. Please be a good brother and sister and do not have any arguments.”

Maria slouched into the seat, saying nothing, but she was very sullen towards her brother. She now realised that others might also think she was crazy if she talked about Semaine.

When Semaine awoke, it was dark. He sensed that Maria was asleep. This was a good time for him to reflect on his journey so far, to be clear on the choices he would need to make, with Maria’s help, to find a way of becoming a chameleon again and to get back to the rain forest. What he knew was that he’d blended into Maria when he’d been disturbed by what he now knew was a dog called Vito. How could he reverse the process? That was the question. He’d tried visualising himself on Maria’s hand, but that didn’t work. Nor did his attempts to blend onto the material on which she was lying.

I'm missing something, thought Semaine. *Something simple, something easy, but what is it?*

He listened to Maria's breathing, shallow and relaxed. As he did so, he felt himself relaxing and again he slept. His last thoughts were of the practice that he and Maria would have to do together, so that they could communicate easily and effectively with each other to find the answer, the key to his freedom.

It was daylight when he stirred into wakefulness. He slowly took in his surroundings through Maria's eyes. Something was wrong—Maria was tense. He saw a woman that he hadn't seen before and knew it was Maria's mother. As he listened to the conversation, he realised that she was communicating the tension.

"We can't stay here with these storm warnings," she was saying. "The hurricane is expected to reach us by mid-afternoon. Maria, we have to go into the hills as soon as your papá gets back with supplies."

"What's going on?" Semaine asked.

"I wondered where you were, Semaine," said Maria out loud.

"What did you say, Maria?" asked her mother.

"Oh—nothing, Mama," she replied.

Maria's mother watched Maria quietly, remembering the conversation she and her husband, Enrique, had had about the strange behaviour that had started while they had been away camping. Maria was definitely distracted—as if she were talking to someone else.

Just then Ramón jumped into the conversation. "Maria's got a secret, Maria's got a secret."

"Shut up Ramón," shouted Maria anxious to stop Ramón from saying anything further.

Maria's mother didn't need this right now. "What secret?" she said.

With a voice rich with sarcasm Ramón replied "Maria has a chameleon in her tummy; like that's real… She's losing it mama, honestly."

"Liar, liar." shouted Maria, lunging at Ramón as if to grab him. Ramón dodged out of the way running towards his bedroom laughing.

“Stop it.” Maria’s mother shouted. She certainly did not need this right now. She pushed her thoughts about Maria to one side as she focused on what needed to be done. “I will speak to you both later. Right now we have much to worry about.”

While Maria, her father and brother had been enjoying the forest, a storm of uncommon proportions had been building up way out to sea. By the time they got back, late the previous evening, the wind was starting to lash the coast, bringing strong waves and declaring its intention to show Mother Nature’s raw and savage power.

“Where is papá?” Juanita asked. “He should have been back hours ago.” Ramón came back into the kitchen. “Have you and Ramón got everything packed and ready to go?”

“Yes mama,” said Maria.

Ramón looked up from where he had started stroking Vito in the corner of the lounge. “Yes mama.”

A gust of wind, a forewarning of the hurricane to come, hit the house. The walls groaned and the shutters shook. They looked at each other anxiously.

Semaine was picking up the tension, yet feeling calm. All his years in his native forest had taught him that when things were going wrong, calmness was essential. His recent experience was strong evidence of this. Maria, feeling his calmness, let her own tension ease.

“What can I do to help, mama?” she asked.

“Nothing for now, Maria. Papá will be home soon, and then we’ll all know more about what we need to do next.”

Maria looked at Ramón and putting aside her annoyance pulled on Ramón’s hand. “Come on, let’s double-check our bedrooms.”

While she was doing this, she quietly explained some more to Semaine about what a hurricane was, what it would mean to the town, and about the plans her mother and father had made.

Some years earlier, when Juanita and Enrique had been children, a hurricane had hit their small town very hard. Of all the buildings in their town, only the church had survived without major damage. Even allowing for the church being a possible haven, she and Enrique knew that they wanted to take other precautions. Because of where the town was situated, and the rocky and hilly ground on which their houses were built, they couldn't build an underground cellar for the family to hide from a storm. After much searching, they'd found a cave in the nearby hills that could be a safe haven if they ever needed it. Over time, they had squirreled away basic supplies, some old collapsible camp beds, and first aid. They visited the hideaway only occasionally, to make sure that it was clean, tidy, stocked with some firewood, and that their provisions were still safely stored away at the back of the cave.

The essentials they needed now were water, food, and light, warm clothes. The town's strongest building, the church, would already be filling up with people. While their town was small, maybe two thousand people, it lay only fifty miles from the major city of Huelva on the coast and about 80 miles from Sevilla. Both areas boarded the Costa del Sol, a 120 mile stretch of coastline. Because the brunt of the storm would be felt closer to the main cities, particularly Huelva, they suspected that a number of people might escape into the countryside for safety, until the storm passed.

Semaine learnt that while the town would receive the fringes of the hurricane, the sea-driven waves and funnel effect of the winds through the surrounding countryside would cause the most damage to the town. He could see the good sense that Maria's mother and father had applied over the years in preparing for just such an emergency.

The front door flew open as Enrique burst into the room, the wind almost tearing the door from his hand. He forced the door shut behind him. The mother and father hugged, acknowledging each other, and then bringing the children in close he let them all know what was happening.

"Okay, family," Enrique said. His tone was serious as he outlined the position to them.

Semaine listened intently, recognising similarities to his own mother and father.

"This is what's happening," he said. "We have no transport. The town is overrun with vehicles from the big city. It's full of people trying to escape the storm. I had to leave our jeep in the town and walk home. The church is full up and looters are breaking into the shops for supplies. People are really afraid for their own safety and that's making some people violent. We'll trust our house and possessions to God and leave now through the back door. The supplies we have in the cave will have to do. The storm's expected to peak tomorrow and start to settle the day after."

He paused for a moment, his face creased with concern. "Because our Jeep is trapped in the town," he continued, "we have a seven mile walk ahead of us. It'll take us two or three hours given the terrain, and we can feel the wind already. We will need extra clothing; we'll rope ourselves together and leave immediately. Remember, we must always support ourselves and encourage each other. If anything goes wrong, we tell each other and help each other. Okay, any questions?"

Maria's mother told him what they'd done and they quickly made choices about what else to leave behind. Within minutes of his arrival, the family slipped out the back door and made their way towards the meadows behind the town that would lead them into the hills and to their safe haven.

At midday, the sky was dark as twilight. Without mishaps, they'd reach the cave by mid-afternoon—about the time the hurricane was due to reach their town. They reached the outskirts and hurried on, into the countryside. In the open space, the wind's increasing strength forced them to lean into it, only just keeping their feet. The rope between them provided a small sense of security as they fought their way towards the forest. Already, the howling wind was flinging debris from the town, which they narrowly managed to avoid.

Semaine was intent, alert to his surroundings and aware that he had knowledge about forest craft that might help his friend and his new family. He sensed the uncertainty and trepidation that created a fear driven by nature's fury. With relief, they finally reached the shelter of the tall forest trees—trees that were also starting to feel the wind's ferocious energy.

He listened to Maria's thoughts as they moved forward, feeling her concern for the situation and her family. They'd been on the move for over an hour, without talking—Maria's father was setting a fast pace, intent on the safety of the cave for his family.

The ground was rising sharply and the air turned dark yellow with approaching rain. Semaine listened carefully, attuned to the sounds of the forest. He knew that the animals would have already sought shelter, aware of the storm much earlier than man. He thought he sensed something else, though: a caution in the air that had nothing to do with the storm, almost a disquiet. He let his consciousness drift into the forest's presence, searching for the feelings of other life forms. He sensed only silence, and Maria's thoughts listening to his feelings, already a familiar, comfortable sensation.

He let himself become one with the forest again, sending out a silent cry for help.

Oh, spirit of the forest, guide my friends, through me. Tell me the path; show me a sign to help us to safety.

Semaine again felt the silence as the group moved through increasingly rugged and demanding terrain. Where were the animals? Even if they were hiding from the storm, he should still be able to sense them, but there was nothing. Danger was brewing—but what was it? Even Vito was restless. For most of the journey, the dog had stayed close to Maria's father and now whimpered and twitched. Semaine recognised the signs that Vito was expressing his own anxiety. Through Maria's eyes, Semaine watched the surroundings for clues. The family hunched against the wind, roped together, picking their way past boulders on the tree-dotted hillside. Rain lashed the forest, drenching their bodies and adding to the hardship of the journey. The hill steepened even more, the ground muddy with water running down the slope. Semaine's senses were heightened now, focused on water, mud, and slope.

At once he knew what it was.

"Maria!" he shouted. "The hill's going to slide any moment—we must move off the slope to that ridge *now*!"

By now, Maria trusted Semaine implicitly; she felt the truth of what he said.

"Papá, Papá! The ground. We must go over there." She started scrabbling to the right of the slope, only to be pulled up by the rope that bound them.

"Maria, calm down. We're nearly there. Hurry up," said her father.

"Semaine," Maria said, "Papá's not listening."

"Stay calm, Maria," said Semaine. "You must convince him."

"Papá," Maria said urgently, "The ground's going to move. I just know it, *please* Papá, let's go over there first."

Vito was barking his alarm.

The rain came down in torrents and the wind bent the ancient trees with nature's force. The whole family was soaked now and both Maria and Ramón were shivering.

Enrique knew that speed was imperative, delay life–threatening, yet there was something in the way Maria spoke. "How do you know, Maria?" he asked.

"I just know, Papá, I just know. Please, Papá, *please*."

Her parents glanced briefly at each other. They knew a detour was risky, and yet…

"Okay, let's go," her father said, leading the way.

Semaine was quiet, attentive to nature, but was able to send a warm feeling to Maria for her faith and effort.

The noise deafened them as they scrambled towards the ridge on the side of the slope, avoiding the small rivers that now raged down the hillside. Instead, they clambered through bushes and over boulders that sapped their energy. It was taking longer than Semaine had thought to reach safety. His every sense was attuned to the land—and then he felt it. Only the slightest of movements, but Semaine knew what was about to happen.

"Run, Maria! Tell everyone to run! We won't be safe until we can get to the ridge over there."

His urgency was clear. Maria started running, pulling her mother forward and pushing Ramón in front of her.

"*Run, run!*" she shouted.

Her father turned and saw what Maria was doing. He too felt the urgency and as he turned to start running, he heard the land rumble. Over the noise of the storm, the land cried out its pain, its anger, its frustration and then her father knew. Landslide.

The ground shook as the world took on a new danger for the family. Maria's father tugged on the rope as he forced the pace faster.

"The ridge, we must reach the ridge," shouted Maria.

It was still about four hundred meters away. On another day, at the local park, it might take a minute or two to cover that distance. Here, with hurricane-force winds little dulled by the gully, dense bush to navigate, and the ground shaking like a level six earthquake, Enrique knew it would be close.

With the ground shaking, they could barely stand, let alone run. They were all falling over, getting up and falling over as they struggled forward. The distance between her father at the front and mother at the back was only eight to ten meters and Maria's father knew that they all had to be safe.

Boulders and sludge, dirt and debris were now crashing down on the hillside. Ancient trees were ripped from the ground and snapped like twigs as the mountain changed its shape. In moments, the landslide would reach their part of the hillside. The ground shifted beneath their feet as they pushed towards the ridge.

They were just breaking free from the main danger area, near the edge of the landslide, Enrique had already reached a tree by the ridge, when he heard a scream. Whirling, he saw his wife being dragged by the ground as it slid downhill. The rope tightened. He threw himself at the tree, his hands clawing the bark. The whole family was now strung out, Maria and her mother hit and pushed by the landslides tide of debris.

Enrique strained with the rope and prayed the tree would hold. Ramón was now only a meter away. Vito crouched next to Enrique, his concern obvious as he watched the life-and-death struggle of his family. Maria and her mother were scrabbling to keep their balance, the mother winded, and the clouds of dirt suffocating.

Semaine focused intently on calming Maria, urging her forward. Ramón had reached his father's side and together they hauled the rope closer. Only two meters now, and Maria would be safe.

The bank gave way beneath Maria's mother.

She screamed. Maria felt white pain as the rope cut into her, the weight of her mother falling back into space. Enrique and Ramón watched, helpless, as Juanita, like a rag doll on the end of a string, was flung violently by the moving forces of nature.

"Maria!" cried Semaine, "Climb to the tree. Help your father and Ramón save your mother. You can do this."

Inch by inch, with her father and Ramón pulling and Maria dragging herself forward, she reached the tree. Her mother was unconscious now, her body dangling on the end of the rope, was still being battered by the sliding hillside. Maria gathered her wits and turned to help her father and Ramón as they dragged their mother towards the safety of the tree.

The storm raged on around them and yet they were oblivious to the roller coaster of destruction as they fought with nature whose death grip on Juanita seemed to strong to resist. The wind had strengthened; the landslide and hurricane competing for who was the stronger of nature's elements. The air thickened with dust and dirt, they fought to breathe, and still the landslide was not yet done. The ground still buckled, shook and jumped, jerking against them as they tugged on the rope, and yet they knew that their only chance to save Juanita lay in those slender strands of rope in their hands.

Gradually they drew Juanita's dead weight up and then over the lip of gully. No sooner had they breathed a sigh of relief than the ground gave way again and the momentum and weight of Juanita's body snatched Maria away from the tree. In response, Enrique threw himself to the other side of the tree and bracing himself, took all the weight. The breath was knocked out of him as he was yanked against the tree. His body bursting with pain, he fought to hold on, the rope wrapped around his arms and shoulders, with the tree acting as a brake—but for how long? Ramón's grip slipped as Maria's weight dragged at him. His feet found a newly exposed root and he pushed against it, unwittingly helping his father in their life and death struggle. Maria, stuck between the two, realised with terror that the ground below her was starting to slip. She looked up at her father, pleading; their eyes locked and Enrique knew he dared not move an inch.

Semaine could only be a voice of calm. There was nothing he could do. Feeling Maria's pain and anguish, he quietly urged her on. Enrique was now working an inch at a time to draw his family towards him. Again and again he strained backwards with the rope then, moving his hands, grabbed a little bit more and strained backwards yet again. Freed by Enrique's work, Ramón swung around to help. The ground beneath Maria shook as it started to give way. In front of her, another tree root exposed itself. She grabbed it and for the first time was able to take some of weight from her father. The pain tore at her waist, her mother still hanging limply from the rope tied around her. Enrique saw a ghost of a chance as he and Ramón anchored the rope more firmly around the tree. Releasing himself, he leapt over Ramón, grasped a tree root, and started to take Juanita's weight off Maria so she could slowly move towards the tree.

With her hands around the tree root and her father taking the weight, Maria watched the ground fall away beneath her. The rope was secure, braced between the roots and the tree, Enrique, Maria, and Ramón now had a better chance of getting Juanita to safety. As Enrique dragged her towards them, Maria found enough slack in the rope to turn and help. Ramón was also pulling now and through the dust, they finally saw Juanita emerge from the chasm below.

Bit by bit, they edged away from the precipice. Enrique was deathly tired.

So close, he thought. He had to reposition himself: with the bank giving way and the roots exposed, the tree was no longer safe, yet it was still their only chance.

"Maria, Ramón!" he yelled, "wrap the rope around that root and hold on tight." As they obeyed, he lowered his wife so that the rope took the strain. He leapt back to the children, grabbed the rope, and began a straight tug of war. They dragged Juanita over the edge of the bank, past the tree roots and finally Enrique reached down, released the rope, grabbed Juanita, lifted her up and staggered away from the tree and onto the ridge. With a crash, the tree toppled into the newly formed ravine.

The children gathered around Enrique as he lowered his wife gently to the ground. Huddled over Juanita, none of them noticed the deathly quiet that had settled over the hillside. The spent landslide and the eye of the storm had conspired to turn off the noise like a tap turns off water.

Chapter 5

Enrique cradled Juanita's head in his lap and whispered to her that they were safe now. He stroked her hair and gently felt for broken bones. Her breathing was shallow and ragged—he knew that without the shelter of the cave and warm clothing, she might not survive the night. More than that, he knew that her life signs were dangerously low and there was no way he could get her to a hospital. Maria's father reached out for Maria and Ramón, and pulling them close, he held them, telling them how brave they were and that they would need to stay strong as they still had some way to go. He spoke calmly, oblivious to the tears coursing through the dirt on his face, and prayed silently that the landslide had left the cave intact.

While Enrique examined his wife, Semaine reached out to her mentally. His consciousness probed her mind, searching for her life force as she lay unconscious. He knew how close to death she was. He could sense, too, the love of her family that permeated her body.

"Maria," said Semaine, "put your hand on your mother's forehead."

Maria reached down and Semaine felt the connection between himself and Juanita strengthen as Maria's hand touched her mother's forehead. Enrique observed them closely. He knew something was happening with his beloved Juanita, but what? Vito put his paw on Juanita's foot as he sought to give her comfort in the only way he knew.

Maria's mother was dreaming. Her body had sunk into a mode of recovery so natural and instinctive for humans who've been traumatised. As she dreamed, she sensed that her daughter was close and something else—a stranger, not dangerous—somehow safe. Then she felt rather than heard the words.

You are safe now, the family is well. They love you so much. The voice calmed and comforted her. Warmth rushed through her body, carrying a realisation of love, hope, and faith.

"Who are you?" she asked quietly and cautiously.

"I am Maria's friend, Semaine, and I am here to let you know how safe you are. The landslide has passed and soon we will be going to the cave. The rest of the family is safe."

The energy flowing through Maria's body strengthened as Semaine allowed himself to conduct the energy of the land, the forest, and the very air they breathed. He focused this loving and healing energy through Maria into her mother. Then words unbidden came through him. It was like someone else was talking.

"You are part of a world of beauty. The love of the earth and the sky is here to help you heal. Please," he said tenderly, *"please, openly receive this love, this energy, this healing, for it is a gift of love and life."*

Juanita heard the voice and felt the energy. Through a haze of subconscious awareness, she heard herself say, "Thank you, Semaine, friend of Maria, for your visit. I welcome and receive your gift." Her voice, quiet in Semaine's mind, was tired and relieved, with that strength of character he often saw in his own mother.

Maria felt her hand pulsing, a heat she could not describe, a love overwhelming in its intensity. She thought she saw the faintest glow around her mother's head, like a weak torch in twilight. She heard the faint buzz of conversation and knew that Semaine was looking after her mother. Her mother was safe: she relaxed a little.

Enrique and Ramón watched, both knowing that something special was happening and sensing that peace and quiet were important right now. Enrique wondered at the faint glow he thought he could see around Maria's hand where it touched his wife's brow. Vito, through his gentle contact with Maria's mother, sensed a pulse of healing energy and felt the same peacefulness.

Semaine knew he had done all he could.

"You are greatly loved," he said. "Be well, you are safe now."

He drew himself gently back into Maria's consciousness, tired, yet confident that Juanita would be all right.

Maria stroked her mother's brow. Her breathing relaxed as she lay. The family watched her eyelids flutter and her eyes open. She gazed up at them lovingly, closed her eyes, and went back to sleep. In the stillness, the family felt close.

Enrique was both relieved and mystified. Another tear rolled down his cheek, relief at knowing his wife and children were safe for the moment. This was not the time to seek answers to his questions—the time for action had come again. Steadying himself for the next part of the journey to the cave, he gazed around and realised that the apparent stillness was increased by an outcrop of rock on the ridge behind the hill. The reality of their predicament following their narrow escape became very clear as the devastation confronted him.

Trees had snapped in two. The hillside they'd just climbed was no more—just a jagged scar that would take many seasons to recover. They weren't safe yet, despite the sudden calm after their escape and the rescue of his wife. As they relaxed from the immediate danger, so their awareness of the storm returned.

Semaine, receiving messages of gratitude from Maria, also knew they were far from safe. In this terrain, they were still badly exposed. Maria had said that because of the weather, their body temperatures were low and Maria explained that something her Papá called hypothermia could make them very ill. Semaine also sensed Enrique's concern.

Enrique knew they now had to follow the ridge in the deceptive dusk. The way would be treacherous. He was also concerned about being able to stay on the path towards the cave. The stillness was starting to disappear as the storm came back to haunt them. Its intensity was increasing; he knew they could easily miss their haven if he wasn't careful. As he picked up his wife, Maria watched with concern and Semaine, through Maria's eyes saw the love of a husband for his wife.

Enrique started walking up the side of the ridge.

"Come on kids," he said, "let's go find the cave."

They were close, he knew—maybe a mile or so, then back across the top of the hill that had borne the landslide. *Thank goodness for the windbreak caused by the ridge*, he thought.

Maria and Ramón watched their steps carefully, following their father. Now Maria brought up the rear. Trusting his instincts, Enrique led them away from the ridge, across the gully, looking for the signs that would lead them to the cave. Enrique knew with certainty that safety was close but now the wind was back with a vengeance and without the ridge to protect them, they were again exposed to nature's fury. Vito, who had been to the cave many times with Enrique, now led the way, grateful to be able to help. The trees were familiar, the shape of the land and the approaching hillside welcoming.

Semaine's mind was highly attuned to the surroundings. He felt the family's strength and the love that bound them. He felt the land, the air and the wind, the fury and beauty of nature. He felt the cocoon of time in which the family travelled through peril to safety. His mind caressed the surrounding wilderness, searching for signs of danger. All was quiet as nature's children—the unseen animals, birds, and insects of the forest—waited for the storm to pass.

Then they were there. Vito barked to indicate a barely discernable opening that led into the hillside. Semaine's instincts found no forms of life inside as Maria's father gently lowered his wife to the ground and searched the cave. Enrique lit a storage lamp and a soft glow welcomed them in from the night. Semaine felt relief as Maria and Ramón helped their father set up the camp stretchers and build a small fire. The cave was well protected from the atrocious conditions outside and the light was only visible from right outside the cave. The ceiling's natural slope moved the smoke up and out to the darkness.

Maria's mother lay sleeping, relaxed on a camp stretcher. Ramón was also asleep, while Maria snuggled up next to her father, who was holding his wife's hand. Vito curled up quietly at Maria's feet. Semaine listened to Maria's thoughts.

I hope Mama will be all right, thought Maria. *I've never told her how much I love her, how glad I am that she is my Mama. I'll be really helpful to papá and Ramón to help Mama get better. Please God, let Mama get better, I love her so much. Papá and Ramón were so strong and brave. Even Vito, dear Vito, was good.* She stretched out one hand and stroked Vito's head, scratching his ears the way he liked. Semaine also felt a fleeting contact with Vito. He was still cautious of Vito given that it was his fear of Vito that had caused him to blend in the first place. Her other hand gripped her father's; through the constant touch, Semaine felt her father's concern.

"Maria," said her father, "I don't know what happened out there. All I know is that it helped, perhaps even saved your mama's life."

With his arm around Maria's shoulders he sensed her drifting off to sleep. He couldn't hear her thanking Semaine for his help and support, nor could he hear Semaine's gentle sleep messages to Maria and to him through Maria's touch. He just knew that his family was safe as he drifted off to sleep.

Semaine longed to sleep himself, but tired as he was, he knew he was experiencing something unique, something that might help him in his quest to return to his own being. In the quiet his loneliness also returned like an old friend to haunt him. As Maria and her father slept, the links that held Maria, her father, and mother were open; each held the other's hand with love and trust and openness. As Semaine lay in the silence, a new consciousness reached out to touch him. It was the only other person who really knew he existed: Maria's mother. Her quiet murmur probed the silence.

Are you there?

Semaine wondered whether to respond or not.

"I sense you're there," her thoughts said gently. "Can you talk to me? I am Maria's mother, Juanita, and I want to thank you for your help earlier. I know it's because of you that I'm alive."

"How did you know that I was real?" asked Semaine.

Juanita was quiet for a moment. Then she said, "When you came into my body through Maria, even unconscious, I knew my daughter was near. I felt this energy burst through me, love and warmth. It was as if the universe and I were connected. In that moment, I felt so keenly aware—like an energy surging through all of the cells of my body. I felt you talking to me. I knew the truth of your love for me and I felt my family's love. I felt my whole body centre and calm and heal while I listened to you."

"How can we talk?" asked Semaine. "I'm in Maria's body, you are in yours."

"Somehow our energies are touching—through my husband, and Maria," said Juanita. She felt Semaine's confusion and waited while he collected his thoughts.

"I want to go home to my family," he said, "I'm in Maria's body. I don't know how I got here and I don't know how to get out."

To Juanita, Semaine sounded like the young frightened creature that he was. Her heart went out to him. All was quiet and still in the cave. Maria and Enrique, unaware of what was unfolding through them, slept deeply and peacefully.

"You have a wonderful family," said Semaine quietly. "It reminds me of my own family."

He sensed the warm feelings Juanita directed towards him. He drew closer, in his mind stretching out a small padded foot towards an outstretched hand. They touched. He felt loved and safe, as if drawn into a big loving hug. His fragility and uncertainty were enveloped in that loving embrace as if by his own mother. His sense of peacefulness increased as he slipped into a deep, deep sleep.

Some instinct woke Enrique. He lay quiet for a moment, his mind recalling events of only hours before. He quietly eased himself from Juanita and Maria and made his way to the cave's entrance. He could feel his exhaustion and his normally upbeat nature was replaced with bleaker thoughts. Their best laid plans were in disarray; safe for the moment but without certainty. In the dark a wry smile crossed his face as he recalled the old saying "We are not out of the woods yet."

What next? he wondered as he turned quietly back into the cave.

Chapter 6

They awoke to a time of quietness. The silence after the ferocity of the storm was something very powerful. As each awoke, they lay still, listening, thinking their own thoughts, sure in the knowledge that they had all been close to death. They had also grown closer: the danger that affected them all had drawn them into a closer, loving understanding.

Maria lay in her sleeping bag cocooned from yesterday's events. As she lay there she sensed a change in her, but what? It was a small niggle. Something was different, but like an illusive butterfly, the answer would not settle long enough for her to figure it out. She eased herself from her sleeping bag and made her way over to where her mother was resting quietly.

While Maria was stirring Semaine wondered about the night before and the touch he had felt from Maria's mother. He'd now conversed with two humans and been deeply affected by them. He also noticed that a new feeling touched his consciousness—different to his sense of Maria. He mentally searched his surroundings. Something had changed. Maria bent down and looked him in the eye.

"Maria!" he said. "Have I escaped back into my real form?"

She appeared not to hear as her hand reached out to touch him. Semaine couldn't feel the hand. For a moment, fear set in, then in the background he heard the murmur of language, of conversation. He relaxed his mind to focus on the murmur and heard, "Morning, Maria, my dear. Thank you for your help last night. Maria—I met your friend, Semaine."

Maria was silent for a moment, then, "How?" she asked.

Her mother explained how Semaine had helped her and how they'd talked.

Semaine's anxiety rose. He was no longer in Maria's body and the thought scared him. How had he changed to where he was now? Juanita was explaining what had happened and how deeply she was moved by the experience. She touched Maria again, saying how her experience had reinforced the great love she felt for her family. Both fell quiet for a while. Semaine thought about the moment when he'd blended into Maria and the similarities between the two occasions. Maria bent down, kissed her mother, and wandered outside to see what her father was doing.

In the silence, Semaine finally spoke.

"Hello."

Juanita jumped, looking around. "Who said that?" she cried.

"Don't be alarmed," said Semaine softly, "It's me, Semaine."

"But how?"

Semaine explained what he thought had happened. "It was when I was asleep," he said. "I remember we were all holding hands and I think it was like when I blended into Maria's body—only this time I moved from Maria's body, through her father's body, into yours."

Neither spoke for a time, lost in reflection.

"I mean you no harm," said Semaine at last. "I really do need your help to get home to my family."

"I know," said Juanita, sounding both certain and cautious—certain of what was happening; cautious because she was part of it.

She realised that she would have to talk about it to her husband. He was always supportive and understanding. This time though, after everything that had happened, she wondered if he would think her crazy.

"Do you think he'll understand?" asked Semaine.

"You can understand my thoughts," said Juanita.

"Well yes. Maria and I used to have thinking conversations quite a lot. I can hear your thoughts like they're my own."

Juanita considered a moment, then said, "Now Semaine, I need to make a rule with you, okay? The rule is this: there will be times when I won't want you to be listening to my thoughts. It might be when Enrique and I are having a quiet conversation, or helping the children with their homework, for example. So I'd like us to have a signal for this quiet time. Maybe a word we can both use to tell the other when we want to have some privacy. Is that okay?"

"That sounds good," said Semaine. "And I'd like to know when it's okay to talk again. How about the word 'forest'? Then I know I can go and think about my family and friends, and the forest I love so much."

"That sounds like a good word," said Juanita. "And I'd like to suggest the word 'friends' when it's okay to talk again."

He liked this, because it could apply to both of them.

Then she said, "Semaine, thank you for listening to what was important for me and helping me to find a way that supported both of us."

The word 'forest' had reminded Semaine of his home. "Juanita," he said, "I do want to go home—I want to work with you, and Enrique and Maria, to understand how we can make it happen."

Juanita thought about the love Semaine had for his family and she knew that whatever it took, they would help the young chameleon to get back to his home and his family.

Enrique was overwhelmed with relief at having Juanita safe. He had not had much time to think as the day had mainly been busy making sure that Juanita was comfortable and rested. And then there was cooking and managing campsite tasks with the children collecting more firewood. This was not easy as the weather was still making things difficult. In the afternoon he had taken Vito and Ramón to look at the hillside where the landslide had occurred and to assess the impact on their return journey.

When he returned he found that Juanita had made a move from the camp stretcher to sit by the small campfire. That was a miracle all by itself.

Now as the day drew to a close he had more time to reflect on what had happened and how lucky he was that Juanita had survived. He also knew that something was different—first Maria and now his lovely wife. She sat beside him, the warm embers of the fire crackling softly as the children slept. Enrique listened intently and as Juanita talked and a new and unexpected turn of events unfolded before him. The story of a chameleon called Semaine inside of his wife was almost too strange to comprehend. But then, he reflected, the last twenty four hours had been very intense and well, different in to many ways to count. He took his wife's hand, gripping it firmly, lovingly, not doubting the truth of her words. Looking into her eyes he said quietly, "What can I do?"

Juanita knew then why she loved Enrique so much.

"I don't know yet," she said. "But we did get through the storm and we'll soon be able to go home. We can plan a trip to the forest for Semaine then. For now though, I just want to be with you, enjoy our time together. Tomorrow will be a day for planning. Tonight's a time for togetherness."

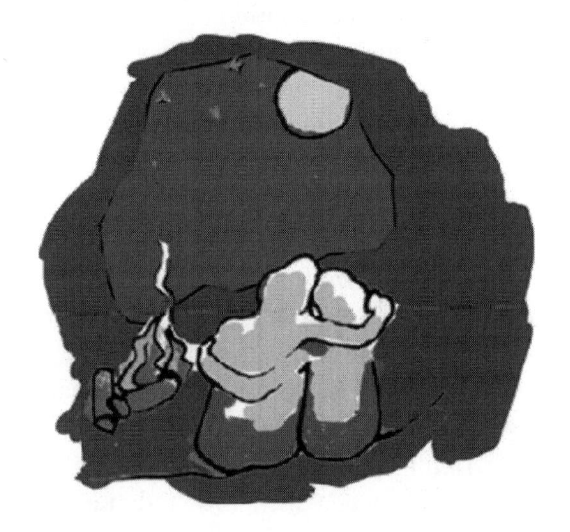

Enrique put his arm around Juanita's shoulders and pulled her close, his gaze shifting to the dark sky outside the cave. Tomorrow would be another day, but he knew their journey was far from over.

Chapter 7

It was wet and stormy when Enrique returned to the cave from the countryside the next morning. He had been on an early morning foray with Vito and he returned with disquieting news. The lack of food and shelter had forced more marauding bands into the countryside.

"I can see them from a distance. Fortunately we are higher up but we will have to be very quiet and very careful. We also need to get back to the town and we can only do that trip without rushing. I think we should leave first thing tomorrow, allowing plenty of time for rest stops."

The previous night Juanita and Enrique had discussed the return journey and they both felt that an earlier rather than later return would be better. Juanita's health was important, and they wanted to return to the town to have Juanita looked at by the doctor and also see how they could help their neighbours. The complication of people in the countryside who might harm them was something they had not considered in great depth.

"Today we will get things ready and early tomorrow morning we will leave for home." said Enrique.

Also not helping was the weather. The aftermath of the hurricane, torrential rain, would make the journey more hazardous.

During the day Juanita rested while Enrique and the children managed most of the tasks. Enrique gave Ramón the important job of guard duty. He was to keep an eye on the surrounding landscape and let them know if he spotted any strangers. Enrique thought they were out of the way enough to be safe… but just in case. He also had them keep the fire small to minimise any smoke being seen. Warmth was critical but so was survival.

It was during this period that Semaine thought about his own predicament. He was non-plussed. His plight was now moving to the bizarre. Just as he was understanding Maria, a twelve year old girl, he now had a new human to comprehend – an adult female. Like Maria, Semaine sensed a good heart in Juanita. That however, he realised was not the point. Having a good heart might be reassuring; it did not however solve his problem.

He took time to also talk to Juanita about finding "himself". He went back over the events of the past two days but nothing obvious jumped out at either Semaine or Juanita. Their conversations turned to other areas of being a "human" and while troubled by not resolving his personal issues, they were enlightening for Semaine. They discussed the planet, love, anger and different aspects of humanity and the world of chameleons. Semaine knew his journey was difficult and challenging—he was, after all, still a young chameleon. Barely in his teens, his tough exterior had only just begun to take on a new texture, grown out of practice and experience which, if he were lucky, would lead to maturity.

The new perceptions he was absorbing intrigued him. His horizons were being broadened by touching humanity and by his experience in this strange adventure.

In the afternoon, Enrique and Maria helped Juanita up on her feet and to take some encouraging steps. It was important for her to test her walking ability. She was still stiff and sore and winced a lot when she moved. With frequent rest stops they felt that Juanita would make it. Enrique had thought about making a sled or a hammock to carry her but the terrain was too uneven until they reached lower ground.

It was during the brief walk that Semaine's heightened senses recognised the return of wildlife to the forest.

"Juanita, tell Enrique," said Semaine, "that I can sense wildlife but no other humans."

As night drew in, Enrique knew they had done all they could.

The next morning, the rain had lessened as Enrique led the family away from the cave. The start of the journey would lead them to the top of the ravine caused by the landslide, and then branch off into the countryside. He had already decided to stay well away from the ravine for the rest of their journey, and to use terrain where the trees were still standing and their root systems were still binding the earth together. The biggest unanswered question was the repercussions of the storm. They knew the wildlife would be looking to resettle their homes in the surrounding countryside and that, just like the landslide they'd already experienced, the aftermath of the storm might present fresh dangers for them. Then there was the town. None of them knew how badly the town had been hit, and damaged homes were always going to be an open invitation to the unsavoury elements of society.

As Semaine watched from behind Juanita's eyes, he felt the sense of excitement and anticipation that infected the whole family. Even Vito barked and scuffled more boisterously than usual, sensing the mood of the family and recognising perhaps that they would soon be going home.

After Enrique had set the route he let Juanita take the lead. Because of her injuries, she would set the pace. Ramón followed with Maria just in front of her father. This time, they didn't need to tie themselves together. They hoped to get back to the town by mid-afternoon.

When they reached the top of the ravine, they could see that the scarred hillside that had caused Juanita's injuries would take a long time to recover. Debris from the landslide rested over a large area at the base of the hill and the scar face itself still looked unstable.

As Semaine surveyed the devastation, he felt nature's pain and recognised nature's cycle. His father used to say to him, "Semaine, watch and adapt like nature—nature adapts through its own beauty and violence. Nature always adapts. And because of this, nature becomes even more beautiful. Learn to be responsive to change, Semaine, just like nature."

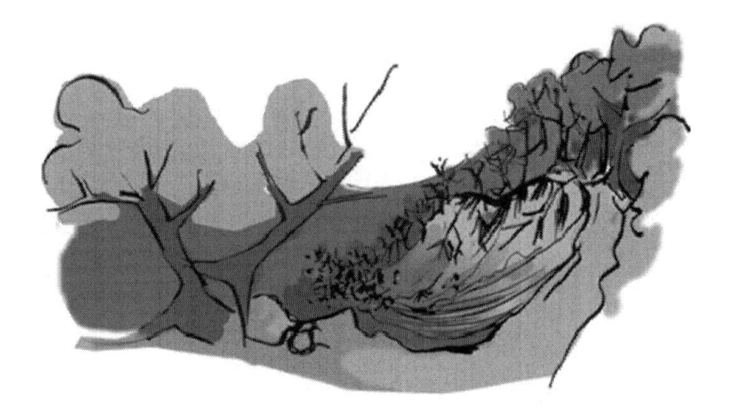

Now that Enrique knew of Semaine's ability to sense other life forms, Enrique had asked for Semaine to keep him and Juanita informed if he picked up any signs of danger.

Semaine reached out with his senses as the family picked their way slowly to the lowlands. He felt only the breeze, the rain and the whispering movement of the branches and occasionally animals seeking out their habitats. The silence though was uncanny.

Juanita followed scrub and bush whenever possible—it was important not to advertise their presence any more than was necessary. Every thirty minutes, the family stopped for a five-minute break, and for lunch they took a full hour. This way, they kept a steady pace with little stress and more relaxation. Enrique and Juanita knew this was important. If they were forced to return to the cave, they would need their strength later.

This was the third day since the storm had driven them to the safety of the cave. As they passed through the ravaged countryside, passing pieces of roofing material, stray clothes, and a car lying sideways smashed into the base of a tree, the storm's violence became more and more apparent.

Shortly after lunch, they drew in sight of the town. Semaine was quiet and watchful. The lack of forest life had tempered his thoughts and his senses had started to pick up human life signs, although they were not close. He spoke quietly to Juanita about the animals' absence, and about the human life signs, which she passed onto Enrique.

As they threaded across the fields, detouring around debris, they saw their house—or what was left of it. Even from this distance, they realised that most of the roof was missing.

Then just as they were to cross the open field behind the house Semaine sensed humans.

"Tell Enrique to wait," he said, "there are humans nearby."

After relaying Semaine's message, the family slowly retreated into the shade of the nearby bushes and waited. Then without warning a group of four men also crossed the field from the opposite direction. They were carrying sticks and even from a distance they carried an air that said – *street gang.* The group stopped and then gathered together. They pointed at different houses and were obviously discussing their next move.

The family remained still. Enrique was quietly stroking Vito's head and willing him to remain quiet. From their style of clothing and the way they carried themselves, Enrique could tell they were not local. He remembered Juanita's comments about what Carlos had said. This must be one of those gangs from the larger cities, forced into the countryside by the storm.

The group suddenly turned with intent and started moving towards their house.

Chapter 8

Enrique could feel himself getting cross as he watched the group circle their home. One of the group walked up the steps and used his stick to push open the front door. Juanita's arm reached out to touch Enrique's shoulder.

"Wait," was all she said.

Then a shout came up from one of the men as he ran to the house next door. The others followed. From out of the house came old Mrs Alvarez. She had been their neighbour for as long as they could remember. She had lost her husband many years ago and her family had all shifted away over the years. She had watched the children grow up and while she was gruff and cranky, she was also someone they had grown to love.

It was easy to see that the gang were taunting her. She waved her walking stick at them, obviously telling them to go away. Enrique could only imagine her courage. Enrique felt Juanita's hand on his shoulder, but his sense of injustice was also simmering.

It was when one of the gang reached forward and pushed her to the ground that he could take no more. He leaned towards his wife and whispered "I love you." And then he was gone. Vito was hot on his heals. For the moment the element of surprise was with Enrique. While not a tall man, he was lean and fit and fast. He crossed the field keeping low bushes and his house between him and the gang. He hoped the drizzling rain would also mask his approach. As he passed his house he picked up an old pipe from the ground and launched himself into the group going for who he thought was the gang leader first.

Standing on the edge of the group, the pain of the pipe hitting his back was the first sign that they were not alone. Dropping to one knee Enrique then took out another gang member by hitting his shin with the pipe. Screaming with pain the second man dropped to the ground clutching his leg. Enrique knew his only chance was to disable the gang quickly. It was his only chance on the back of his surprise attack. Two down, two to go. Now it was not so easy as the other two left Mrs Alvarez and started to circle Enrique. As one of them started to move in Vito arrived at full speed snarling ferociously as he knocked a third gang member over. As the gang turned on the new threat Enrique seized his chance swinging the metal pipe hard, catching another gang member in the chest. The sickening crunch as the man went down told its own story. Without waiting Enrique moved onto the man being pinned by Vito smashing the pipe into the man's ankles.

Vito and Enrique now stood side by side. Vito's teeth were bared, his rage apparent. It was then that the first man Enrique had hit, the one who seemed like the leader, got to his feet, pulling out a gun and swinging it towards Enrique. Vito leapt as the gun went off and then he crashed to the ground. Enrique charged the man with the gun. A second shot rang out. The noise was deafening as he hit the man with his shoulder, using his weight and momentum to lift him off the ground and crush him against Mrs Alvarez's house. The man dropped unconscious to the ground.

Enrique's head was ringing from the gunshot. He dimly thought he could hear sirens in the background.

"Is that it?" he thought.

Turning slowly he knew he was going to be too late to react if there were any more to deal with. The last gang member had also partially risen. From the shape of his leg, Enrique could tell it was broken. The man was grinning as he also lined up a gun at Enrique, knowing that he was now in control.

"Goodbye you stinking fool," his voice was cold. It was as he was pulling the trigger that a spade hit the side of his head sending him into the dirt, the gun firing aimlessly into the ground nearby. Mrs Alvarez stood puffing and then leaned on the spade for support.

Enrique collapsed to his knees his head ringing as he looked up, his head spinning. He thought he saw a police car before his body caved in and he crashed head first into the muddy ground, unconscious.

This was all too much for Semaine. The aggression and violence was something he was not used to. In the same way he was not used to tragic loss. First he saw Vito crash to the ground and then Enrique. By now, Juanita, her own pain forgotten, was also on the move towards where her husband lay, her voice screaming in anguish.

Semaine reached out his mind towards the two life forms. Of the two, Enrique's heart was beating strongly. It was Vito that was losing his life force. Semaine reached out to Juanita. "Enrique is alive," he shouted, "but Vito is going to die unless we can get to him quickly."

But Juanita was not listening to anything other than the need to be with Enrique. As she reached the scene of the fight she turned towards her husband. She was met by Carlos Barthez and his deputy Atilio. Carlos was their long time family friend who was in charge of the local Municipal Police. He had arrived as the last gunshot had rung out. Juanita did not stop to chat. As she ran past him she yelled. "Look after Vito."

"Enrique," she cried out as she reached him and lowered herself to her knees beside the still form of her husband, tears starting to stream down her face. The rain was still falling but unnoticed by Juanita.

"Juanita, its Semaine. Listen closely, Enrique's life form is unconscious but his heart beats strongly. He will be alright. His body is adjusting to the pain."

Even though she heard the words all she could see was her husband lying motionless in the mud.

Semaine spoke quietly and yet deliberately, he knew he had to reach Juanita in a deeper place. "Juanita! Remember your recovery on the hillside. Please just listen to me. Please put your hand gently on the back of his neck."

There was hesitation, confusion and then comprehension as ever so slowly Juanita reached out to Enrique, her hand trembling, fearing to touch and yet willing herself to do so. His skin felt warm as she made contact, first with her fingers and then with the palm of her hand.

"Good," said Semaine, "now, just send him your love."

Once again Semaine reached inside and this time it was easier. Working through Juanita's deep feelings for Enrique he once again called on the healing powers of a loving creator.

Deep in his unconscious state Enrique could sense a new presence.

"Enrique, I know your Spirit can feel this moment. It is Semaine. The same Semaine that Juanita talked to you about. I am the same Semaine that helped to heal her when she was on the mountain."

Enrique replied hesitantly, "Semaine, my family, Vito. Am I dead?"

Speaking reverently Semaine said "Juanita and the children are safe and you are very much alive. Now Enrique, please open your heart and receive the gift of this healing love energy to speed your recovery." Semaine felt the energy flowing through him.

Once again Semaine felt words come through him. *"Enrique, you are part of a loving universe and you are so loved by your family, your friends and your God now reaches out to bring you His healing. This healing love will restore and enrich you. Please openly receive this gift."*

Enrique felt a rush like nothing he had experienced before. It was as if every cell in his being exploded with joy. He felt an incredible realisation that he was truly loved. He deeply felt God's presence and he knew with a certainty he had never felt before that everything would be alright.

Very gently Semaine said "Rest now Enrique." He knew he had done all he could and he withdrew himself back into Juanita.

Juanita by now was beside herself. She had been the recipient of Semaine's gift of healing love and now had been a support for it, just as Maria had been only days before. Tears coursed down her face.

"Thank you Semaine, thank you with all my heart."

Semaine was tired but knew he could not rest yet. "Take me to Vito," he said.

While Juanita and Semaine had been with Enrique a lot had been happening. Carlos and his deputy had called in for help and had already disarmed and immobilised the gang. Enrique's attack had lasted minutes and yet had inflicted broken and fractured bones.

Maria and Ramón had gone straight to Vito and had been joined by Carlos. Both children were visibly upset and as Juanita approached she and Semaine could see the pool of blood that lay under Vito's still form. They had started to put a shelter up for Enrique and had already erected a small shelter to protect Vito from the elements. They were reluctant to move either patient until medical help arrived.

Semaine asked Juanita to get close to Vito. As she crawled under the makeshift shelter he then said "Juanita, do the same for Vito as you did for Enrique only this time put your hand on his side."

Juanita did as she was instructed and again she felt warmth as Semaine reached out for Vito's spirit. "Juanita, I do not know if this will help or not. Vito has lost much blood and his life signs are very, very weak."

"Vito, can you hear me." There was only stillness and silence. Semaine felt his own emotion rise up. He had never witnessed anyone sacrifice themself before and yet here, in this animal, Vito had expressed a depth of love for his family that many would have shied away from. Semaine felt the words again spring to his mind. *"Vito. Your sacrifice was not in vain. Enrique lives."*

A voice reached out to him. “Are you from the forest?”

“Yes,” said Semaine surprised by the response, “it is my home. One day I want to return there.”

“I thought so,” said Vito. “Am I dying? It is dark, is it night already?”

“Vito, you are very weak. I don’t know if I can save you but I will try.”

Juanita could feel the energy start to build. In some ways it was the same, in other ways stronger, perhaps because of Vito’s injury. Ramón and Maria watched distraught. Maria knew what was happening while Ramón, once again could only watch and wonder. Mrs Alvarez was looking on through eyes that had seen a civil war, while Carlos looked on confused by what was happening. Normally he was in command but now he was, like Ramón and Mrs Alvarez, standing on the sidelines knowing without understanding that something profound was occurring.

The pulse of energy flowing through Juanita was now so strong that her hand felt hot and her senses were also becoming overwhelmed.

Semaine again felt words come through him. *“Vito,”* said the voice, its tone rich and deep. *“You have honoured your family and your creator today. Such love for others is rare. You were prepared to give the ultimate sacrifice. Now Vito, please open your heart, your mind and your spirit to this gift of healing love energy. You must trust this energy and this love. Your creator loves you and now he honours you.”*

Semaine, in the heart of this moment was also feeling overwhelmed. His senses were heightened as he felt energy pour into Vito. This was a step up again from what had happened to Juanita and Enrique and he knew that it was because of the seriousness of Vito’s wound. He also knew he had done all he could. Just as he was about to withdraw a weak voice reached out to him.

“Semaine, thank you. I… I sensed you. I know… what you did for Juanita. I just wanted to… say thank you for every…thing.” Vito’s voice faded as Semaine’s emotion finally caught up with him. He realised that if he was human, he also would be crying.

“Rest now Vito.” he said quietly as he withdrew back to Juanita, exhausted by his effort.

“I have done all I can Juanita. I must rest now.”

Juanita could tell from Semaine’s voice that he was tired and spent. Again Juanita thanked him, marvelling at what had just happened. She knew that Semaine was now asleep and that it was time again for the next step, making her family safe. She turned to them and said “Semaine said he has done all he can.”

Maria and Ramón reached out for their mother. Carlos was looking bewildered. “Who is Semaine?” he said.

“Let us talk later,” said Juanita sidestepping the conversation, “for now we have other things to do.”

Atilio came up to talk to Carlos. “The doctor is on her way and should be here in a few minutes. I also asked for her to ring the vet about the dog. They are organising an ambulance but in light of the last few days, it might take a while as it will have to come from Cadiz.”

“How are our, ah, friends?” said Carlos.

“They are fine, just grizzling about their pain.”

“Juanita,” said Carlos, “Why don’t you take the children and look at your house. Mrs Alvarez, would you be able to make us a drink perhaps.” Carlos knew that any form of activity now would be a helpful distraction until more help arrived.

Mrs Alvarez nodded and wandered towards her house. Carlos gazed after her as Juanita and the children moved towards their house. He had no idea how long Mrs Alvarez had lived in their town, but it was clear that she was not going to be thrown out by a big old hurricane or a street gang.

As Maria and the children turned their attention to their home, they saw that the wind had blown in the windows and a tree had been pushed through the side of the house where the children’s bedrooms had been. They reached its broken walls and stood beside it, each struggling in their own way with the destruction of their home.

Juanita spoke quietly. “Let’s look inside.”

They found that Enrique and Juanita’s bedroom and the kitchen were the only two rooms still roofed, and the kitchen windows remained intact. The children’s bedroom walls had been pushed in by the tree and stood open to the elements. They were a mess. Maria’s bed had been taken by the storm while Ramón’s lay crumpled under the tree. Puddles of water lay throughout the house, so they couldn’t switch the power back on. The family area was filled with debris. The toilet, with a door and no roof, was surprisingly serviceable.

The children, though dazed by the events outside and the destruction of their house, seemed very resilient. Juanita was sifting possibilities and solutions to their predicament and also seeing past times of laughter and sadness. She was seeing her family in another setting: one where intact walls had cocooned their family and encompassed their dreams. Shaking her head she again took charge.

“Okay,” said Juanita. “Children our options are limited for the moment. We need to find out what is happening for Papá and Vito. We also need to find out what’s happening in town. We do have one bedroom, the kitchen is intact and we have some supplies and bedding; so we can stay here if we need to.”

Juanita, who was glad to have something to focus on, then said, “Why don’t you two see what we can actually use here at the house. Find a pen and paper and make lists. While you are doing that I can find out what’s happening in the town from Carlos.”

Both Maria and Ramón thought this was a good idea.

“All right then,” said Juanita, “I will be back soon. Call me if you need me. Mrs Alvarez is making drinks. I will call you when they are ready.”

They all embraced before heading off to do their separate tasks.

Juanita found Carlos by the police car. He explained how many people had left towns and cities and been trapped on motorways and roads while others had sought refuge in the church.

“It’s not good,” Carlos said gravely. “Most of the town’s facilities were destroyed. We have no power and it won’t be restored fully for at least another week. We have some generators on loan from Sevilla. There’s a town meeting tomorrow morning at eleven o’clock to discuss our future. We have aid coming from Cadiz and Sevilla and relief aid from agencies is arriving daily.”

“Have many been hurt?” asked Juanita.

“Only a few. In fact, we were worried about you and your family when you weren’t at the church. Oh, thank God for the church. The building is still standing and most of the town’s people and their families managed to get into the church and the school before the worst of the storm hit the town. But there were people badly hurt on the motorways and some are still missing.”

“What about your family and your home?” asked Juanita quietly.

“Junior and his mother are alright,” replied Carlos. “They’re at the church. Our home is still standing, but with no roof, so until then…”

“Are there food supplies, and blankets there?” asked Juanita.

“Yes. It’s the central distribution point for the whole town and one of the generators is positioned there for emergency power.”

Juanita looked at her watch as Mrs Alvarez came outside and called out that tea was ready. Just then a car came down the road.

"Ah", said Carlos, "Doctor Angelica Morales. She arrived yesterday from Cadiz and has been working non-stop since. I hope she was able to get Sancho, the local Veterinarian, to look after Vito." Sancho Alberto del Castillo or Sancho for short, like Mrs Alvarez had lived in Zalamea la Real for too many years to count.

They went to meet the car. A middle aged women got out of the passenger side while an older man got out of the drivers side.

"Sancho, Angelica, thank goodness you came so fast. Come this way. This is Juanita Rosa Hernandez. It is her husband Enrique who is lying here and Sancho, Vito is over there."

The two doctors wasted no time and split up to examine their respective patients. Juanita called out to the children to go to Mrs Alvarez's house and said she would meet them there.

Doctor Morales called Juanita and Carlos over. "He is very lucky. There are powder burns, on his head. He must have been very close to the gun blast. The explosion of the gun and the resulting noise has literally knocked him out. I suspect some mild concussion but he does not need to go to hospital. I would suggest that you move him to a quiet room and he will sleep this off. Also, some paracetamol for any pain after he wakes up would be good."

Juanita's relief was evident and she said "Thank you Doctor. The bedroom in our house is serviceable. We can move Enrique there for the time being."

"That sounds fine to me." said the Doctor. "Now I must attend to the men who caused all this."

While Carlos called over Atilio to discuss moving Enrique, Juanita quickly went to see Maria and Ramón. She explained that their father would be alright and would just need some rest and that she had no word yet on Vito. She asked the children to stay with Mrs Alvarez until she came back. She then rushed over to the house to make sure the room was okay while Carlos and Atilio lifted Enrique carefully and moved him to the bedroom.

Once he was made comfortable, Juanita felt relief surge through her. Losing Enrique was not something she even wanted to think about. Through the window, Juanita could see Dr Morales was crossing the yard, moving between gang members when another Police car arrived. Carlos said "Juanita, I have to get the prisoners back to the jail in town after they have been looked at by Doctor Morales, so let me and Atilio see to this while you get an update on Vito."

As Juanita emerged from the house she found Sancho bending over Vito. Turning towards her he said "It is not good. The bullet hit Vito in the chest and exited through the rib cage. His life signs are very low. I need to get him to the surgery to operate and Juanita, he might not survive the trip into town."

Juanita's face was resolute. "We have to do everything we can. Vito saved Enrique's life today by taking the bullet meant for him."

Juanita again sought out Maria and Ramón and explained about Vito's condition. "I know you are both upset, however, for now we must be strong for Vito and Papá. I am sorry I have to leave you here for the moment, however, Papá is resting and I have to deal with the doctors and the police."

She was right. Both children while knowing their father would be alright and would recover were distraught about Vito who had been such a part of their lives while they had been growing up. She gave them both a hug and sent them back to Mrs Alvarez and then went to find Carlos.

Carlos had two of the gang in the back of the police car. They were the two least injured and were being sent to the jail. The other two were subject to broken bones from Enrique's onslaught so Doctor Morales was still carrying out temporary triage for their journey to the hospital in Huelva.

Juanita went back to sit with Enrique and it was about an hour after that that Dr Morales appeared.

"Hello Juanita. Now come into the other room. I came to do a final check on Enrique before leaving. I have just been talking to your boy Ramón who was telling me that only two days ago you were very badly injured."

"Yes that's true; we were caught in the storm and a landslide. I am very lucky to be alive."

"Indeed you are Juanita." said the doctor and as she put her medical bag on the kitchen bench she said, "Can I have a quick look at you while it is quiet."

The examination took only a few minutes. "Juanita, did you say you were caught in the landslide?"

"Yes. In fact I was knocked out and if Enrique and the children had not pulled me from the ravine, I am sure I would have died."

"I have seen severe trauma from countryside accidents before and yet your injuries seem to be almost healed. I have never seen such rapid recovery."

"So I am okay?" asked Juanita.

"Yes you are. When this is all over, would you mind if we had another chat about this?"

"Yes of course," said Juanita, secretly wondering how she would handle that conversation.

Doctor Morales examined Enrique and then said "Alright then. Juanita, he is quite stable now. All you can do is let him rest. I must go back soon as I have been paged for another emergency."

Juanita walked the doctor back to Carlos. Sancho and Vito had gone in one of the police cars and the last two prisoners had also just departed for the hospital for further treatment.

Juanita had already decided to stay at the house with the children. Even allowing for the rain which had lessened slightly, it was now four in the afternoon and moving Enrique and the children to a new environment would be difficult.

Juanita said, "I will share the two houses with Mrs Alvarez and that way we can look after Enrique."

Carlos said he would stop by first thing in the morning to see if they needed anything and, if the family were up for it, he offered to pick them all up for the town meeting on the way back to the church after his rounds in the morning.

"One last thing," said Carlos. "Just be careful. As you have seen, there are a still people moving through houses looking for valuables. My patrols won't always spot them or deter them, so keep a watch and be safe." Juanita watched Carlos and Doctor Morales drive off.

Turning back towards her house, Juanita's mental checklist was in full swing.

Husband knocked out. Children with neighbour. Vito in hospital. Semaine asleep. No power. What next? She made her way back to the house desperately tired but knew for now she could not afford to relax. Rest would come later.

Chapter 9

It was dark when Enrique woke. He lay still listening to the sounds as his mind started recalling events. His family! Oh no. Enrique jerked upright realising and remembering what had happened. As he did so pain shot though his head and he collapsed back on the bed.

"Enrique," a voice wafted across his mind. Juanita. My God, you're safe he thought.

"Lay still." Juanita said gently, "Everything is okay," Again relief surged through her as she reached forward to hold his hand. Even though Doctor Morales had said Enrique would be alright, she needed her husband awake and lucid to believe it.

"What happened," asked Enrique, his voice raspy after waking up from his deep sleep.

"Well, it's now eight o'clock in the evening. We are in our home, well in the bedroom anyway. The rest of the house is a bit... ah...messy. Vito is in hospital, but no word yet. He took a bullet meant for you and he is in a bad way. You were knocked out by the gun going off next to your head. You are very lucky. Semaine did some of his healing on you and Vito but Semaine has been asleep as well. I think the healing activity really tires him out. Maria and Ramón are with Mrs Alvarez who is fine. I have done some tidying up but it is awkward with the rain. Tomorrow we should head to town I think."

"It must have been very difficult for you. I'm sorry I rushed off like that but it made me very angry the way they were treating Mrs Alvarez..." said Enrique, his voice fading just a little.

Juanita could see that Enrique needed more sleep so she briefly added some more detail about the police, the doctors,

Mrs Alvarez and how the children had been excellent during everything. She talked about the town meeting and the offer Carlos had made.

"I would like us to go," said Enrique

"I think so too but for now you must rest. Firstly though, the doctor wanted you to take some paracetamol. I have it here. Then I will quickly get the children over to say goodnight. They have been very worried for you."

Juanita returned a few minutes later with the children and Mrs Alvarez in tow. "Papá," the children said in unison crowding the bed to give him a hug. Maria was crying and Ramón was trying to be very brave. They, like Juanita, would only believe Enrique was alright when they saw for themselves. After a few minutes Juanita asked them to make way for Mrs Alvarez.

"Enrique," she said, her voice thick with emotion. "I have no words enough to thank you for what you did today. I have lived through a Civil War and suffered the death of loved ones. What you did for me today was beyond most people's reason. I need to tell you that I am so very, very grateful." Then her voice changed again to the gruff Mrs Alvarez they knew. "Next time… remember I am old and you are young and that your family needs you… and I can take care of myself!" With that she winked at him, turned and said, "Come children, your Papá needs some more rest."

As they were leaving a police car turned up and parked between the two houses. Atilio got out and came to speak to Juanita and Mrs Alvarez,

"Hello Mrs Alvarez, Mrs Hernandez. Carlos asked for volunteers to stay on patrol near your house during the night. We all volunteered and then made a roster. I am here till midnight when one of the other officers will come and relieve me. Mrs Hernandez, what your husband did today was very brave and this is our way of showing our thanks and our respect."

Juanita and Mrs Alvarez were very grateful. Juanita kissed the children goodnight and made her way back inside to talk to Enrique, only to find he was already fast asleep.

Juanita crawled onto the bed beside her husband. She was also deathly tired. As if the trauma of the past few days had not been bad enough, the emotional roller coaster of the day had taken its toll in a completely different way.

His name being repeated quietly had finally jerked Semaine from his sleep. Disorientated it took a few seconds for him to adjust.

"Semaine." said the voice again

"Hello." said Semaine quietly.

"You did well today Semaine." The voice paused then continued. *"You will recall that I told you earlier that you would be tested and also that love would be important. Today you instinctively found a way to provide a healing loving energy from all that IS to make a difference."*

Semaine remained silent.

The voice continued *"The journey is not yet over Semaine. You have many gifts that have been given to support you. You will need others soon."*

"Will I get to go home?" asked Semaine.

"Every journey has a destination Semaine. Some are not as you expect."

More riddles thought Semaine. "I understand, I think, but will I get to go home?"

In the stillness remained only silence riddled with Semaine's unanswered questions.

Chapter 10

The family were waiting, wrapped in warm clothes, when Carlos arrived to take them to the town meeting.

Between Enrique and Semaine wanting to learn more, Juanita was feeling more than a little hassled. Normally it was Ramón and Maria having sibling spats. Having two supposedly mature intellects hounding her was a new and not necessarily pleasant experience. Bless Mrs Alvarez she thought, for she had taken over the children as a grandmother would.

Carlos also brought news that the operation on Vito was finished and Sancho had asked them to come and see him after the town meeting. They headed towards the police car for the ride into town. Semaine recognised that they were again getting into what Maria had called a car and knew he was going to have another speed experience. In some ways he was looking forward to it.

Looking out through Juanita's eyes he was again subjected to watching his surroundings move at what felt to him like breakneck speed, even though the car was forced to move slowly through the streets. As he squeezed his patrol car past obstacles in the road, Carlos also mentioned that the roads around the town had been so affected by debris after the storm that road usage was restricted to emergency services and essential supply transport.

As they moved towards the town centre, they saw the full extent of the damage to the community. Most of the devastation had occurred in the main street of the town. Small buildings had been flattened by the storm. One shop had two cars pushed through its walls; a tree was lying through the middle of another, its branches stretching half into the street. The church looked largely unscathed—itself a miracle, given the surrounding devastation. Many of the people were already inside the church when the family arrived with Carlos and cried out with welcome as they recognised Enrique and his family. Word of his heroic act had spread and many went out of their way to shake his hand.

Semaine's involvement with the family hadn't prepared him for the sheer number of people at the town meeting. The church hall was packed. Conversations babbled on every side—to Semaine, the noise was deafening, quite the opposite of his treasured forest. He felt crowded, his natural instincts to blend and hide heightening.

"Shh…" murmured Juanita, sensing his unease. "It's okay, there's no danger. No one's going to hurt you."

As the perceived threat subsided, Semaine began to watch, like a detached observer, the unfolding drama of the townspeople and the meeting. He knew how he'd feel if his forest had been destroyed or if anything was to happen to his family, so he could only guess what it might be like for those who'd lost both.

Juanita told Semaine that there were at least three hundred people there. Semaine said he couldn't imagine a meeting of three hundred chameleons, which brought a small chuckle from Juanita. A series of bangs from the front of the church brought silence. A group of men and a woman sat at the front and an elderly-looking man started talking.

Juanita told Semaine he was the *Alcalde.* He is like a mayor of the town and the Alcalde with other people elected by the towns' people organised and ran things for the town.

"My friends," began the Alcalde. "As you know, our recovery as a community is very much linked to the support of our friends." He indicated some of the people at the front of the room and continued. "Father Xavier, who has put a roof over our heads and with the help of God, has kept us safe from the storm. Mr. Dean William, our visitor from America, who represents the International Aid Agencies. Dr. Lorena Ortega, who is on our Municipal Council and who has been treating those who have been injured and sick. Again we must thank the additional medical support we have received from Cadez, Huelva and Sevilla. Mr. Juan Castillo, from our government, and finally Carlos, who has patrolled our streets to keep our homes safe from looters."

Sitting as they were at the front of the room, they looked impressive to Semaine. He sensed an underlying mood in the audience, though he struggled to identify it. The closest he could get to it was a constrained patience. As he surveyed the crowd, he noticed something else about them. Their life forces were visible. He saw whites and pinks, which he sensed indicated calm. Also scattered in the audience were the deep reds of anger. Only when he spoke to Juanita did he realise that she couldn't see them. Juanita was torn between wanting to understand what Semaine was talking about and listening to the meeting.

Semaine watched the result of loss being turned to blame and frustration through to anger. These were the deep reds in the audience—those whose families had been most affected. As the meeting continued, the townspeople's emotions flowed relative to the needs of their families. He saw, too, the life force of those in the front of the room, who would provide aid and support in the aftermath of the storm. Plans were unveiled to provide temporary shelter while houses were rebuilt; to restore power; to clean up the town; to support law and order. They aimed to bring a degree of normality to the lives of the townspeople over the following months.

From Semaine's limited knowledge, he could see that there had been a disaster and that everyone working together would bring the necessary solutions for people to rebuild their lives and the town. So his confusion grew when those 'red' elements in the crowd became demanding and angry. They wanted the work done faster; they wanted more compensation. Bewildered, the chameleon watched as the mood of the audience changed, driven by an angry minority.

He told Juanita what he was seeing and pointed out where it was most red. Juanita, still listening to the increasingly heated exchange, recognised that the people in the area Semaine had pointed out had indeed lost much because of the storm. Juanita spoke to Enrique, who'd also been observing the mood swing in the room and becoming frustrated by people's responses. After listening to Juanita, Enrique decided to speak out to his fellow townspeople.

"Alcalde," Enrique shouted above the crowd. "Can I say a few words?"

Heads turned in his direction. The crowd grew quiet. They all knew Enrique and his family. Giving Juanita's hand a quick squeeze, Enrique made his way to the front of the room, turned to face the crowd, and paused. His eyes roamed over the people as the room became still and expectant.

"My friends," Enrique began. "I'm deeply troubled. We've had our town, our lives, badly damaged. All of us, in some way, have suffered loss. But God has favoured us. We're alive and God has sent people to rebuild our houses, feed us, shelter us, and restore our power."

He paused and looked at the areas Semaine had said were hotspots, which tallied with his own view.

"I know you all. I thought this town was tough. One hundred years ago, after such a storm, there would not have been any help. We, the townspeople would have had to do it all ourselves with no power and no foreign aid. And what welcome do we show these people, my friends?"

Many in the crowd were looking down at their feet, ashamed as they listened to his words.

"We have much to thank God for," he continued. "Let us each do our best. Let us rebuild our neighbours' homes. Let us be stronger because of the storm. Let us work together with these people who have come to us with aid. Aid where there was none, my friends."

The crowd remained silent.

"This is a town I am proud to be part of." he resumed quietly. "We've seen each other grow up, been in street fights together as children, seen each other get married and have children of our own. We've been to funerals together and mourned the losses of our family and friends."

Enrique was not a tall man, five foot seven inches with hair that looked like it always needed a comb, but as Semaine watched the quiet man speak words from his heart to his friends, the audience calmed. Semaine saw Enrique's strength and his sincerity. The man's voice reached out to the crowd once again.

"My family and I came close to death in last few days—so close that we felt God's hand on our shoulders. Yet we are here now and we live to fight another day. So let us fight now for each other and for our small town." As he spoke, his voice rose with passion, then he turned to the Alcalde and said quietly, "Let us know what you want us to do. My family will be there."

The crowd was silent as Enrique stepped down and made his way back to his family. Before the Alcalde could say a word, a voice rang out from the audience.

"Alcalde, put down our names as well."

"And ours," said another voice as Enrique reached Juanita's embrace. Through the hug, Semaine felt Enrique's strength of purpose and his belief in his friends and town. Semaine marvelled at the change that Enrique's words had brought to the crowd. Semaine had felt Enrique's commitment to help his friends and had also been empowered by his words. The reds in the crowd had turned pink; the hot spots in the crowd were now wanting to help. The short speech had redirected their energy, by redirecting their thoughts.

In Enrique, Semaine recognised his own father's love and passion, and remembered his father's words. "Semaine," he had said, "remember that all of your actions will have a consequence, so make your actions count. Act for the good of your fellow chameleons and you will make a difference." Oblivious for a moment to the meeting, he sought out his homeland in his mind. Was his family safe? Would he see them again? Would he ever be real again?

"Semaine… Semaine." Juanita's voice reached into his thoughts. "Are you all right?"

"Yes, I'm okay," said Semaine quietly.

"We're leaving now," Juanita said. "We'll come back for another meeting tomorrow, to be allocated some work."

In the following days, Semaine witnessed a blur of activity as the streets were cleared, power restored, and those people who could returned to their homes. Enrique and Juanita were both kept busy doing different tasks every day, joining the children every night. The looting stopped as more people were allocated to help Carlos patrol the streets, everyone taking turns. The patrols were also made easier as people cleared the rubble from the streets. More help and supplies arrived daily at the church and a makeshift town of tents was erected for the homeless. Order slowly appeared out of chaos and Semaine recognised a spirit and resolve in the people, not only to survive, but also to grow stronger. He hung onto the words he'd heard from Enrique: "Juanita," he'd said, "tell Semaine that as soon as we can, we'll return to the forest."

Over the weeks after their return from the cave, Semaine searched for ways to return to his normal self. He'd thought about his initial blend when he became one with Maria and realised that his blend had had one crucial mistake. Instead of blending to match the colour, shade, and complexion of Maria's hand, he'd blended to become *one* with Maria's hand. In doing so, he'd changed from a tangible reality to a presence without form inside someone else's body. What perplexed him was that he had to find a way to change from an invisible presence back to a real form. He had to materialise himself as a complete, separate entity. It wasn't a matter of blending, or of transitioning as he had with Juanita. He knew now he could do that with any life form. That blend didn't give him any control—but it did give an interesting sense of harmony and communication with other life forms, which entranced him. He was still no closer to a solution. He tried imagining himself next to Juanita's hand. He asked Juanita to place her hand on a tree branch and… nothing. He spent countless hours while Juanita slept trying variations of the blend that had transformed him into another state, all without success.

He sought quiet spaces to listen to the voice, which came to him only occasionally in the stillness to reassure and encourage him. Then after a particularly frustrating time looking for the elusive key that would return him to his real self, the voice spoke to him in the still of the night. It spoke about challenges.

"Semaine," the voice said, *"You are challenged no more and no less than you're capable of handling. This is true for every life form on planet Earth. Whether it's a storm, the loss of a loved one, the state of your health and vitality—whatever it is, the challenge is a test of every individual's resolve, and a chance to demonstrate courage and compassion, perhaps in a time of great fear."*

"Challenges come in different shapes and sizes, and mean different things to different chameleons. There is, however, one constant - Change. Change and growth wrought by the challenge may have unexpected rewards and strengths. So embrace change. Allow yourself to be challenged but don't get lost in the challenge. See instead the outcomes you desire and focus your energy with belief and trust towards these ends."

Semaine knew he was being tested and he again sought out the key words the voice had given him—What jumped out more than anything was that *change* is continual, that it would be *challenging* and could bring *unexpected rewards,* but he would need *resolve* and *determination*.

This was empowering. It encouraged him, giving him enthusiasm to keep looking for the elusive key that would unlock the door to his freedom and restore him to the reality he wanted. He wondered about the voice—that strong, resonant voice, which he knew he could trust. Whose was it? The Creator? Was it the God that Juanita and Enrique spoke about and prayed to? It always came unexpectedly and with meaning. It always strengthened him, encouraged him, and gave him a chance to reflect. In its own way, it was another mystery to Semaine.

Something else was also absorbing Semaine's thoughts: what he called his new gifts. Firstly, the way he'd helped heal Juanita, Enrique and Vito was something he'd never done before, but he'd intuitively known what to do. Secondly, there was the way he saw the colours of other people's spirits—what Juanita called their auras. He'd never been able to do that before, either. And thirdly, there was his increased sensitivity to nature. The air, the land, the sea seemed to speak to him. He'd felt the pain of the landslide and the joy inherent in re-growth. The breeze whispered to him of different species becoming extinct and how the earth's reserves were being plundered and the air polluted. He already knew of nature's balance, but nature speaking to him was wholly new.

A perplexing question in Semaine's mind was, therefore: "Why me?"

He had many conversations with Juanita, and through Juanita with the rest of the family. These were both enlightening and alarming. On one hand, he felt the delight of a world viewed through Ramón's eyes: those of a young boy with freshness and energy. On the other, he learnt of people's capacity for both compassion and violence.

He wasn't afraid of Vito anymore. The experience in healing Vito had been done without any thought of fear. He had seen Vito's willingness to sacrifice himself and knew Vito's depth of loyalty to his family. The news they received about Vito after the meeting had been disquieting. Sancho explained that while Vito's operation was complete, recovering to fight another day was a whole different issue. Loss of blood and the trauma had taken a heavy toll on Vito's body. It was incredible that Vito was still alive when he got to the surgery. It was now up to Vito. Over the following days Vito's life signs improved slowly. The whole family visited Vito every day. Each time, Semaine asked Juanita to rest her hand on Vito's shoulder. Through this process Semaine not only continued to support Vito's recovery, he conversed with Vito as well. Semaine had discovered the way Vito loved, cared for, and protected his family.

Also occupying his mind was his weariness. He was tired more frequently and he was noticing that he slept more. It was often after he had spent time conversing through Juanita with other family members or Vito. It was different and yet similar to the exhaustion he felt after he had healed Vito and Enrique.

His tiredness though was pushed aside by his frustration and anxiety. Being with his adopted family invariably led his thoughts in a big circle back to his own family, to his parents and his return to the forest. He was still no closer to solving the puzzle of returning to his normal self and he was still no closer to his beloved forest.

Chapter 11

Over dinner one night, during a brief hiatus in the seemingly continual frenzy of activity, Enrique turned towards Juanita and said, "Juanita, please tell Semaine that I received news today that the roads between the town and the forest have been cleared sufficiently for us to travel safely. If it's okay with Semaine, we can plan a trip back to the forest."

Semaine, listening in to the buzz of family dinner discussion, one of his favourite times, was first stunned, and then ecstatic at the thought of his return. In the family's sudden silence, he felt both their sadness to lose him and their joy for him.

Juanita spoke Semaine's thoughts. "Enrique, Semaine says thank you very much, and he's excited and sad to be going—but he still hasn't found a way to return to his real self."

"I know," said Enrique, "but I feel it's time. We got the Jeep back late yesterday so we have transport and I can arrange for us to all take a two-day break from the work in the town and, well—we'll see. Semaine, my friend, it's up to you. If it's okay with everyone, we'll leave within the next few days."

The news, while bringing mixed emotions around the table, left Semaine pondering his predicament. Once again, he faced the unknown and possible risks. His life would never be the same again and neither would that of his new family. Their lives, like Semaine's, would forever be touched by his miraculous transformation. *Transformation.* The word took Semaine's mind instantly to a new approach he wanted to explore with Juanita. Juanita said she didn't know much about it except that it was when one form became another. "Think about water Semaine. It becomes steam when heated and ice when frozen." She had then suggested that they visit something called a library in the next town and also used something called the Internet. Now that the Jeep was fixed, Juanita would be able to take them. When Semaine mentioned it, Juanita said she would find out if the library had reopened and if so they would go as soon as possible.

It was a revelation for Semaine. The library opened his eyes to the way humans made knowledge and creativity accessible to everyone through books. He'd learnt about books and television from Maria, but he wasn't prepared for the number and diversity of books available even in a small library. When Juanita told him that this was a very small library compared to the libraries in larger centres his comprehension about the size of the planet was now moving him towards overwhelm. He learnt about dictionaries, and encyclopaedias, and then there was the Internet: the whole world accessed through a network of computers called the Internet or World Wide Web. Juanita used the word "technology," and talked about "access to information."

In his world his colony was central to his world. Conversations were not passed over distance, but to each other. Sure chameleons, like all animals, had heightened senses however, this was different in so many ways. It was like the television or the radio, he thought. Unseen behind them were lots and lots of different programmes and he realised that he needed to look at things one piece at a time so he could put it together like one of the jigsaw puzzles Ramón sometimes played with.

And so the library became an accessible resource centre, the results of which further astounded Semaine. It was as if his favourite stump in the forest had taken on a new dimension. His perspective on life and his forest would never be the same. He'd always known he was part of a larger life force, but the sheer magnitude of the planet, the cosmos in fact, left him in awe of the Creator's grand design. Perhaps it did still need the magic of the forest to bring all of the elements together.

Through Juanita, Semaine learnt about his own species and recognised pictures of his own kind, which he pointed out to Juanita with great enthusiasm. He learnt that humans called him a *Mediterranean Chameleon* or a *Chamaeleo chameleon* and that his cousins were spread across different parts of the planet and how many different forms they came in. He also learnt that in Spain and in many other countries he was a protected species.

He learnt about great humans such as Einstein, Socrates, and Plato, whose minds had explored, and given meaning to complex concepts and philosophies about and within a world humans called Earth. Semaine discovered how man had explored the heavens, stood on the moon, and studied the stars. He found out about others, such as Ghandi, Martin Luther King Junior, Benjamin Franklin, Helen Keller, Mother Theresa and Nelson Mandela, whose lives dramatically impacted on humanity.

And this was the tip of an enormous iceberg of human endeavour. Sport, politics, arts, science, theatre, and dance all contained their own heroes. Juanita said that in their Region of Andalucía they also had many famous people like the author Juan Valera who died a long time ago, and Theresa Zabell Lucas who sailed boats on the sea and in her time was one of the best competitive sailors in the world. Semaine thought about his own heroes—his mother and father. He thought about Enrique and

Juanita, the courage and determination they demonstrated and the difference they made in their community.

What made the difference between heroes like these and other people? All heroes had mothers and fathers, like everyone else. Once upon a time, all those heroes were children who played, ran, and had adventures. Was it a vision? An idea? A feeling of what was "right" that inspired these people? And what courage and resolve did they need to support them on their journey? Did they, Semaine wondered, also have a voice that talked to them?

It was after several visits to the library that Semaine's thinking began to take on a new direction. What shaped his thinking more was what had happened when Enrique had protected Mrs Alvarez from the gang, and the confrontation at the town council meeting. They were events driven by Enrique doing something about something for the *right* reasons.

Semaine realised that, without exception, every life form had the opportunity for success. It was the individual who made their choice to act, relevant to their own circumstances. A mother soothing an upset child was as much a hero as a man or woman standing by their principles, or a frightened soldier who saved his comrades.

To act in the moment for the highest good... thought Semaine. *Perhaps that is what is in every moment of every day. To be in life rather than to be an interested bystander. To make life come alive rather than be driven by events.*

Every moment was a choice. To persevere or to give up. To show courage or to give in. To be sensitive or to get angry. To see strength in differences or to follow prejudice. To sacrifice oneself to an endeavour or to take the easy way out. To love or to hate. In each case, both the choice and the consequence belonged to the individual, theirs to accept or deny.

Perhaps the real hero is inside every life form from the time they are born, thought Semaine. *Perhaps we're our own hero just waiting in the wings for the first sign to act in the moment for the highest good.*

He knew that *highest good* was an important key—that in striving to be the best he could be, he'd show values that would benefit and support others. The highest good! His father had spoken about it when he was very young.

"To do something for others, Semaine," his father had said, "carries rewards of unknown quantity. It carries grace and beauty to another and may often have other unexpected rewards for oneself and those others you touch."

The thoughts of his father brought his mind back to the present.

With Juanita he now knew a lot about transformation and metamorphosis. Every day before their return to the forest, he would practice with Juanita but still he was frustrated by the result - nothing! He knew he was missing something simple, but what?

The time was now close to when they would leave for his forest. What if he could not transform himself back to his real self? What if he was forced to remain inside Juanita forever? 'What if's' crowded his thinking. For the moment he was locked in another world. What he desperately sought was his escape. The key however, was still elusive.

Something else was worrying him. His bouts of tiredness had increased. He was getting weaker and weaker with each passing day. At first he had put it down to all of the new experiences, things he had learned and his constant need to change back. It had grown from a small niggle in his mind to something more real. He now realised it was more than tiredness. It was as if his life force was tailing off.

This was a different 'what if?' What if he was dying?

Chapter 12

It was the next morning after the family had scattered in different directions; Enrique picked up by other town helpers and the children to school, that Semaine released his bombshell.

He talked to Juanita about his energy and what it meant the longer he was not his real self. His revelation changed everything. There was an urgency that was not there before. She knew that no matter what it took, they would do everything they could to save Semaine.

Juanita knew that the news would hit her family hard. Semaine's sudden inclusion in the family, his insights, friendship and acts of healing had, without any of the family realising it, created another family member; someone who really mattered to them. It was as if Semaine had become a brother to each of them. As a consequence, the family, already feeling a sense of loss at Semaine's impending departure, would feel a deeper emotion at the thought of Semaine dying.

"Semaine," said Juanita, "I need to see Enrique right now and talk this through with him."

Fortunately, the Jeep was back. A little more battered and worse for wear, but still useable. They made their way to where Enrique was working on the recovery operations in town.

Enrique was visibly shaken by the news. The connection with Semaine was very special to him. In accepting the news Enrique was also clear that speed was an imperative. Both Juanita and Enrique knew that this also involved the children. Semaine was also clear that he was not leaving town without seeing Vito one last time.

"Juanita," said Enrique, "it is still early in the day. If we leave now and get the children and supplies we could see Vito and be on the road just after lunch. That would mean we would be at the campsite in the forest just before dark. What do you think?"

Juanita agreed and Enrique went off quickly to explain to his colleagues that he would be gone for a few days. Then they drove to pick up the children.

At home, while they were getting things ready, talk was subdued as they each thought about the implications of Semaine's predicament. Juanita had been right. The news had hit them very hard indeed.

Through Juanita, Semaine said to them all. "I don't know what is happening to me, but I do know that this time with you and your family has been beyond imaginings. The memories will stay with me forever."

The family headed towards the mountains and the forest, expectant, uncertain, and sad. Even sadder was Vito. This was one trip he would be unable to make. His health had improved slowly but surely and his life signs had become stronger but not enough for him to venture into the forest. They had made the detour to Sancho's surgery so that Semaine could say his goodbyes to the animal who had unwittingly started this whole affair. Through the regular visits, Vito had himself come to appreciate the strange being that lived in Juanita, while Semaine had so much respect for the way that Vito had been prepared to sacrifice himself for his family.

Each in their own way had grown through this unusual experience. None would be the same again. As a family, they were a stronger team. Each, including Vito, had found a way to communicate with Semaine and he with them. The word 'fellowship' is often used lightly—but that best described the family's underlying mood. Together, they were on a quest whose outcome was far from certain.

Enrique parked the Jeep in the same place as on their last trip to the forest. As the family grabbed their packs and made for the camp site, Semaine was already reaching out to the forest with his mind, feeling its freshness and energy, the touch of other life forms, as they went deeper in. They stopped to take in the view at the top of the hill, as special to Semaine as when he'd first seen it. Almost overwhelmed with Semaine's emotions, Juanita steadied herself. Semaine, she'd learnt, was one strong, strong character with deep beliefs and unquenchable curiosity alongside a highly analytical mind. He was also so intuitive that his perceptions constantly amazed her.

She recalled how, when they were in the library one time, they had been talking about the concept of war and she mentioned the crusades of many centuries before. "Do you mean that in the name of God, who is a God of peace, humans will go to war? Do you humans actually learn from your mistakes?" or when they were talking about families it was much more direct, "You mean a family member would not speak to another family member for years and years because of something that was said, because it was easier to ignore the other person rather than discuss it?" and then he had added, "For such an advanced race, you humans are very strange."

Through his eyes, she and the rest of the family had been given a fresh view of the true meaning behind words such as kindness, truth, brutality, war and love. As a result of his closeness and involvement, Semaine had become more of a friend to her than she would have thought possible. Now she wondered about the parting and how it would affect her.

Maria and Ramón, on the other hand, were conflicting stars of studied thought and curiosity, filled with wonder that they might yet get to see their hidden friend at last. For the last two weeks, Semaine had been a voice without a body. They knew what a chameleon was but to actually see their friend would be amazing.

Semaine felt all these emotions as they left the town behind and entered the wilderness of nature. He was reviewing the various things he could try, to transform back to his true state. Something about his transformation into Maria held the secret that would bring him back again.

The restful forest showed little sign of nature's turbulent fury only weeks before. Each of the family felt its peacefulness as they made their way down the trail towards the camp site. For Semaine, the emotion of his homecoming was tangible, the strength of his passion washed over Juanita. His senses sought his chameleon family. Like radar, his antennae sifted through the various species of wilderness life forms he was sensing. Birds and insects abounded—but as yet, no chameleons. Through Juanita's eyes he recognised the scenery his heart had longed for. The various shades of green on green. The mottled sunlight through treetops dancing with the breeze across the forest floor. The rustling leaves as the lightest of breezes carried scents of nature's heaven to Semaine's heightened awareness. But it was more than this. The forest carried the smell of nature. It was still damp and wet from the storm. It smelled fresh. It smelled like home. As they walked into the clearing, he saw, at the far end of the small meadow, covered in sunlight, the old tree stump where his incredible adventure had begun.

As the family set up the camp site, Semaine asked Juanita to take him to the tree stump. Looking through her eyes, he felt the peacefulness of the forest which was in stark contrast to the tension he felt.

He knew he was weaker still. Given everything that had happened and then to die so close to his family. It didn't bear thinking about. He needed to get out of Juanita's body and the fear of failure was now stronger because the stakes had gone up – his life would be forfeit.

Chapter 13

Okay, this is it, thought Semaine.

To Juanita, he said, “You’ll need to rest your hand on top of the tree stump.”

Juanita was already moving towards the old stump. It had snapped about six feet from the ground in some long-ago storm. The base was wide—at some past time, the tree had been majestic. Over time, the sun, wind and rain had smoothed its edges into a platform perfectly positioned to overlook the glade. Juanita pulled herself up onto the stump, a good five feet in diameter. She sat cross-legged, facing out over the camp site, just as Semaine had done all those weeks ago.

“Okay,” said Semaine, realising that he’d picked up that saying from Maria and Ramón. “Okay,” was not a word he had ever used. “Okay, Juanita, can you put your hand on the tree stump?”

Through Juanita’s hand, Semaine let his senses reach out to the wood. He could feel its texture and its grain once again. As he focused, Juanita became aware of what Semaine was attempting to do.

Semaine thought of his own life form. He thought of himself as a whole chameleon. He imagined his long, thin legs and his toes that helped him to grasp branches. He thought of his eyes and the unique vision they gave him. He thought of his tail and his tongue, which he used for catching insects. He thought of his domed forehead and its horns and ever so gradually a picture of himself formed in his mind. When he thought he had a clear enough picture of himself, he mentally projected his image onto the stump. He concentrated with all his strength. He thought of the texture of his skin and how he would feel the warmth of the sun and the touch of the breeze and…

Nothing.

Again and again, he went though the process. Each time he made subtle changes. Each time was the same. The rest of the family were quiet, waiting while Semaine attempted the transition… and still… nothing. On top of which, this mental exercise was tiring him making the concentration more difficult.

Juanita felt his disappointment and frustration, though he'd fallen quiet while he thought. He was missing something, he knew, but what could it be?

"If only I could talk to my parents." he said to Juanita quietly.

She paused. "Do you think they can help?"

"I don't know. But I know that I'm missing a key, and just maybe my father or mother can help."

"Maybe we could find them?" Juanita suggested.

Semaine thought this was a good idea. In the chameleon community, Semaine explained, his father was particularly skilled at blending. While it was natural for chameleons to blend, it was a chameleon law that parents had to equip their children for their future in nature's wilderness. This meant that every parent taught their children, to the best of their ability, how to use blending to survive. What was more, becoming one with their surroundings had given the chameleons a unique awareness of nature and its laws. And so he turned his thoughts toward his parents. His mother whose gentle and yet strong nature complimented his father, who had taught him so much as he grew and been so patient with him. They might hold the key to his dilemma.

"How will we find them?" Juanita asked.

"I'll take you to another part of the forest, where lots of chameleons live, and go to the home of my family," said Semaine.

As the family collected their packs, Semaine added that quietness would help him reach out with his mind to find the life force of his fellow chameleons and his mother and father.

While Semaine was looking for them, he knew that they would be worried for him. "*It'll be good to see my parent's again.*" thought Semaine.

With this in mind, he started to feel the presence of the chameleon life force. After about half an hour's walk, the presence strengthened. Like radar, he sorted them into known and unknown life forces. He called a halt and spoke to Juanita.

"I can feel my mother's life force and that of other chameleons, but not my father," he said. "Maybe the others should wait here while we go see my mother."

Enrique, while reluctant for Juanita to go on alone, realised that the group presence might not help Semaine. After all, chameleons were solitary creatures by nature and the sudden appearance of four humans could be seen as a threat.

Juanita and Semaine went quietly forward, threading their way through the undergrowth as Semaine gave directions. She felt the peacefulness of the place and Semaine explained that chameleons had colonised in this part of the forest for many generations. Its remoteness had been good for them; they'd thrived and been enriched by the distance from predators and civilisation. More than anything, the reflective chameleons had become even closer to nature and to the one life force that permeated all. For this reason, as well, Semaine wanted a peaceful approach—by now, some of the chameleons would have already seen Juanita.

"Over to your left," he said, "about twenty yards away, there's a tree. About ten feet up the tree—there, on that outreaching branch—there's my mother. If you climb up—then when you're close, lay your hand on my mother's back—gently, ever so gently, and I can talk to her."

Juanita was thrilled at seeing Semaine's mother. She'd never seen a live chameleon before. As she drew nearer, the chameleon seemingly materialised in front of her. The tail tightly wrapped around a small branch. The greenish-brown tint of the skin. The bulbous forehead, the eyes fixed and still. The skin was rough as she rested her hand on the chameleon's back.

Semaine's mother had been aware of a strange life form in the forest for a little while. It had come closer and closer and, as was the way of her kind, she'd frozen and blended with her surroundings.

She was astonished when the being came right up to her and in the midst of her confusion and fear, the being suddenly put its hand on her back. From the energy of its touch, so light and gentle, she sensed no danger—and then, something familiar. Something she knew. Abruptly, Semaine's voice burst into her mind.

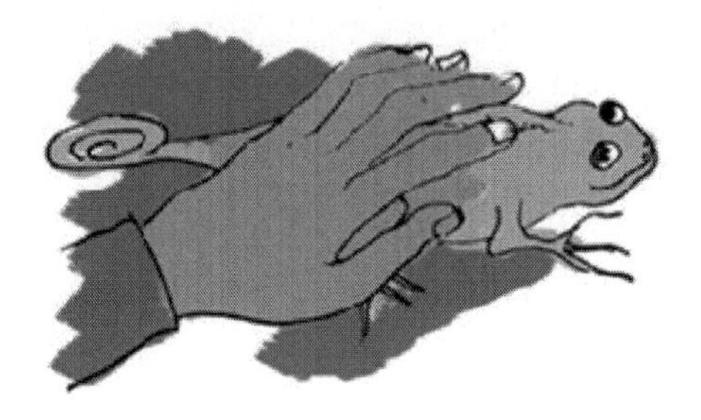

Mother, can you hear me?

Her son's voice—just as she remembered. The chameleon community had given him up for lost, but she and her lifemate had refused to accept it. Even now her lifemate was out searching for his son. She knew the bond between them was deep and her lifemate's sense of loss profound.

Her confusion rose: this was her son's voice, but the being looked nothing like him.

"Mother, its me." the voice said again. "*Please don't be afraid. I'm part of this human being—it's too long a story to tell now but I am trapped inside this human being and I need help to return to my normal self."*

She was silent, still, wondering at the conversation that was going on in her mind. Was this really her son? She had missed him so much. His sudden disappearance had caused so much pain. And now to hear this voice so like her son's.

"How?" she asked. "How do I know it's really you?"

Semaine thought for a moment. "Do you remember when I was very young and one day I tried to get a butterfly cocoon with my tongue? And you told me that inside the cocoon a miracle was growing and that I had to sense and respect the different parts of nature. Do you remember?"

She was stunned. This voice was Semaine's all right. With that realisation came a host of questions. If only Semaine's father were here to help.

Semaine sensed his mother's confusion. "Mother, I need you and father to help me?" While he spoke gently, his mother could also sense his desperation. She realised also that being confronted with this being and her son as one and the same was beyond her ability to be of real help to him.

"I think you need your father for this Semaine. He's out looking for you again, this time to the east. He's been gone for two sunrises—he should be back the day after tomorrow. He's gone to the Sacred Grove, where he used to train you when you were younger. Do you remember?"

"Yes, I do. We have to go and find him. I'll be back, hopefully like my old self. I love you mother."

This was too much for Semaine's mother. In normal circumstances she could look at her son and put out a padded foot to comfort him. All this on top of holding it together while her son was missing and her mate was distraught over Semaine. Her voice thick with emotion, she said "I love you too son. I'll be here when you get back. Be safe, come back soon—I've missed you so much."

Semaine was also affected by the moment. For the last weeks he had been praying for a way to get back to the forest and see his parents, and now that he was this close to his mother it seemed almost surreal.

Forcing himself to be strong he said, "I know mother. I've missed you too. I'll be back soon."

Juanita raised her hand from Semaine's mother's back, knowing how she would feel herself if anything happened to Maria or Ramón. Warming at the thought of Semaine's family being reunited, Juanita made her way through the late afternoon back to her own family.

That night by the campfire, through Juanita, Semaine talked to the family about life as a chameleon: the sense of family and community, their relationship with nature, their part in nature's destiny. He told them the lessons his father had taught him and how he recognised many of his father's qualities in Enrique and his mother's quiet strength in Juanita. The story absorbed Maria and Ramón. Their perceptions of nature were taking a new turn, as they realised their responsibility to nature was global, even while they sat around a small campfire in a forest miles from civilisation.

As the evening drew to a close, their tiredness was caressed by the peacefulness of a quiet forest where life existed in invisible communities. Nature's balance was linked to these small life forms, with no knowledge of humanity but still linked to it. As the opposites of night and day are linked by dawn and dusk, so it is that the merging of difference creates its own beauty.

Semaine couldn't sleep. He was so close and so very, very tired. His patience so far had been rewarded with the conversation with his mother. His mind relived his experience of the day until sleep finally claimed him.

Chapter 14

The day dawned bright and clear and the family maintained their camping discipline of rising early to prepare for the journey. They tidied the camp site with a sense of expectancy and anticipation. Unanswered questions might finally be answered; they might finally see the Semaine who spoke in their minds.

For Semaine, this last leg of the journey meant finding his father. His weakness was still there. It felt tempered by being home and seeing his mother but he knew that he must find a way back soon. Again, he would tread the fine line between belief and challenge. He knew that if he continued to work with the challenge, he would be all right. If he got lost in the challenge, he could slip into the space his father called despair. Optimism would draw him towards his father. The first step, though, was to find him.

The family set off with Semaine guiding them towards the rising sun. Early morning light filtered through the canopy overhead, littering the ground with fairy shapes of light. Every now and then, beams of light emerged like beacons searching for a place to alight, beams of light alive with dancing particles of energy. The forest was also alive with birdsong as nature's wildlife stirred into another day.

Semaine told the family, through Juanita, that they were going to a part of the forest considered sacred by all of the forest creatures. Many of the species living in the forest would go there for enlightenment about issues that affected them. Semaine had been there rarely and each time with his father, never alone. Only selected individuals from each species were allowed to visit the sacred place. He asked them all to reach out their thoughts to the forest as they walked, to let the forest know that they were respectful visitors.

As Semaine led them deeper into the forest, a tangible restfulness touched all of their thoughts. At times, it felt like they were being watched, not suspiciously, but rather curiously. For more than two hours, they tramped, resting when Enrique called for a break. The family was in good spirits and Semaine, although he had not sensed his father, felt confident. He'd noticed many native life forms and he knew that every step brought them closer. He'd led them in a half-circle around the chameleon colony and now they were headed towards the sacred place, in the direction he felt sure his father would have taken, and would return by.

By lunch time they were on the fringe of the sacred place. The stillness was palpable. Semaine asked them to wait there, while Juanita and he went on alone. He still couldn't feel his father's presence, but he knew where to go. Juanita hugged Enrique and the children and told them she loved them. Then the human form of one being and the spirit form of another stepped into the Sacred Grove.

Chapter 15

His son going missing tormented Semaine's father. It was like a deep, fulfilling attachment had been torn away. As a son, Semaine had been mischievous, questioning, pushing boundaries, and an avid learner. Through watching his son grow and being alongside his learning, a bond of special closeness had formed between them. It was a bond that had moved past father and son to friendship and respect.

When Semaine hadn't returned, his father knew something was wrong. It wasn't like his son to be so late. He went searching himself and sent word out through the chameleon community to look out for Semaine. Chameleons had natural enemies, yes, but he couldn't shake the feeling that somewhere his son was alive. He knew that his lifemate felt the same way. He was deeply spiritual and after discussing the matter with his lifemate, they decided that a trip to the Sacred Grove might give them some insight into where Semaine was.

The Sacred Grove had been a special place for many, many generations of chameleons. It was a place where all forest dwellers could come in peace. By unspoken law, the representatives of the different species, even enemies, could come without fear within its confines. It was a place of immense natural power, one of the few points that the Creator had chosen as an eye between two worlds, the physical and the spiritual. A place of peace, harmony and meditation.

Semaine's father was the chosen representative for his community. Occasionally, he brought with him other chameleons in need of answers or healing, and ever so occasionally, he brought Semaine. In this private haven, Semaine's father renewed his faith and reached out his mind to the great protector and provider, asked that his son be kept safe, wherever he was, and that one day he might return safely to his family. The time in the Sacred Grove always seemed so short. He delayed his return, as he always did, hoping that some sign would appear or that the voice would again speak its truth to his heart.

Only once since Semaine's disappearance had the voice come, with its comfort and direction. When his sense of loss was deepest, it had said, *"Trust in him; believe in yourself. He is life and life never ends. Feel peace and strength in these simple truths."* The voice hadn't returned, but Semaine's father did take strength from the words. They reminded him, in his grief, to honour the certainty of belief and trust. So he believed and trusted that wherever his son was, he would be safe and one day he would return.

This visit to the Sacred Grove was drawing to an end. His thoughts turned often towards his beloved Semaine and to his lifemate's continued love and support. He knew it was time to return. As he sat on an old log near the centre of the Sacred Grove, preparing himself for his journey, he became aware of another presence. His rotating eyes made out a tall, two-legged creature. He sensed safeness, and something else, too. Something indefinable, something familiar.

Chapter 16

On entering the Sacred Grove, Juanita knew something was different. There was a silence here she had never felt before. The energy of the place gave a sense of life that almost overwhelmed her senses. Colours turned stronger, sharper. The greens and browns added more shades and blended rather than contrasted - amazing. Then the forest smell added to a heady cocktail; it was intoxicating. The forest aromas driven from the damp musty vegetation were somehow deeper, richer and empowering. Then there was the stillness. It was different from silence.

In all her travels with Enrique, she had never felt a place with such deep peacefulness. Before the children were born, she and Enrique had travelled to the Picos de Europa National Park in Northern Spain. It is vast and majestic and yet powerful, almost foreboding. It was a place she recalled now and then for it had a profound affect on her understanding of nature. But this place, this Sacred Grove, was touching her soul in a way no other place had.

As she walked where Semaine directed, she saw a thousand sunbeams dancing on the forest floor in a joyous dance of welcome, entrancing her with the tapestry of nature and the depth of God's creation.

She was humbled and found herself in grace, thanking God for all her blessings, and especially for her husband Enrique, her amazing and incredible children, Maria and Ramón, and their loyal friend Vito. She drank in the emotions of this quiet grove, aware that Semaine was also moved by its tranquillity.

It had been so long since Semaine had been here with his father and yet each time was as invigorating as the first, refreshing and revitalising. He dreamed of one day being elected the representative of the chameleon community to the Sacred Grove and following in his father's footsteps. In his own right, he would fulfil a destiny he felt awaited him. He reached out into the grove with his senses and felt his father's life force. At once, he directed Juanita's vision, until they could both see the shape of a small chameleon, almost invisible, perched on an old log on the forest floor, watching them. Overjoyed delight, fulfilment, and questions surged through him. What would his father say? What would he think? Would he be able to help?

Whatever happens, thought Semaine, *At least I can see him.*

Juanita approached, ever so cautiously, Semaine's excitement roaring in her mind. When they reached the old log, she laid her hand gently onto his father's back and Semaine stretched out his thoughts towards his father. He could feel his father's life force and his sense of curiosity. He reached further, looking for the murmur of his father's thoughts to connect with. How he loved seeing his father again. Then he felt his father's stillness and acceptance that something strange was happening. Semaine delved deeper and finally knew he could connect.

Semaine's father had been following the progress of this new being in the Sacred Grove for some time, puzzled because it was a life form he had not experienced before but the way it reached out to touch him with its thoughts was familiar. When it came into view, he saw at once that it was huge, and coming straight towards him, but he felt no fear. What was it about this being? He watched as it stretched out an arm and he felt it rest on his back. Then a voice burst into his consciousness.

Father! It's me, Semaine!

He twitched, startled almost into blending. He recognised Semaine's voice—but this strange creature, this being, was nothing like him!

"Semaine? How—? What—?" He fell silent a moment, lost for words, and then with a voice full of emotion said, "It's so good to hear your voice, son. I, we, have missed you so much."

As his father spoke, Semaine felt his father's bafflement, then curiosity, and through it all his love. Stumbling with happiness, Semaine explained his dilemma and how he had come to be here.

"So you see, father, something's missing—and I think you're the only one who can provide the key, so I can return to my normal self. Father, I am also worried because I am becoming weaker and weaker the longer I remain here in Juanita,"

This news hit his father like a bolt from the blue. To be reunited and then have his son taken away permanently was to frightening to contemplate.

"Tell me again, step by step, what you're attempting to do, then show me what you've been doing," said his father.

"All right, father," said Semaine, and he quickly explained how he had been trying to transform back to his real self. When he finished, Juanita moved her hand a little way down the log. Semaine stilled his mind and focused his thoughts. Again, he pictured his chameleon form, his body, his tail, his eyes, and his head. He pictured the texture of his skin, the softness of his tongue, and the curl of his tail. In this strongly spiritual space, he could sense his life force—see in his own mind his chameleon shape on the log. He opened his eyes… he was still inside Juanita.

Juanita felt his disappointment as he asked her to put her hand back on his father's back. Immediately, he felt his father's excitement.

"Son, you're keeping your life force inside the other being. You *are* creating the image of yourself—but to bring it to life, you need to move your life force into the image you've created. That's the final step."

As soon as his father spoke, Semaine knew it was true. That was the missing key, the link to his real self—but how? Each time his life force had moved before it was without any conscious approach on his part. Blending into Maria was an accident and he slept through the whole transition with Juanita. This last attempt had also weakened him further. He needed rest but he knew to become his real self, he had to find a way.

"Thank you," said Semaine, with a rush of love. "I'll try again."

This time, Semaine's father sensed his son's growing exhaustion.

Semaine explained to Juanita what he was going to do, then said, "Juanita—if this works, I don't know if we'll ever speak again. But whatever happens, I want you to take me back to the family, so they can see the real me. Whatever happens, I want you to know how much this has meant to me. You and Enrique, Maria and Ramón have been a second family to me. A family I will always remember."

Juanita could also feel Semaine's tiredness and was choked with emotion. "Semaine, you have been a real friend and we'll miss you. You've given us more than just a gift of friendship. You've shown us a link to nature we'll always treasure. And you, Semaine, you're the greatest treasure. Your openness, determination, love, your special insights, have made a real difference to us." Tears flowed from her eyes. "You've enriched us, Semaine, and we'll always remember you with love."

Moved by Juanita's words, Semaine said quietly, "Thank you, Juanita. Remember—if it works, wait a few moments, then touch my back and I'll see if we can talk."

Juanita promised. Semaine settled his thoughts, knowing that he would need all his concentration, as she again rested her hand on the log, a little way from Semaine's father. Ever so slowly, his mind relaxed and as he did so, the voice came to him once more.

"*Semaine,*" it said. "*Why don't you come into the light? Then you'll be where I am.*"

Semaine was startled. Right now, he definitely did not want another riddle. Come into the light? What did that mean and where was the light? And did that mean he would meet the voice?

Then the voice spoke again "*The light is inherent in all life. It is the space where I am.*"

How strange, thought Semaine. *Did the voice just answer me?*

"*Semaine,*" it continued. "*You have endured many tests to be here, but here is all there is. This moment is your time. The light is where you will find me.*"

Semaine fell silent, confused. "*The light is where you will find me,*" he repeated to himself. "*Step into the light?*"

He was no longer thinking about a transformation back to his real self but rather about the new puzzle that had presented itself. *The voice does seem to like riddles,* he thought. *But why now?* The voice was consistent. It spoke when he needed it. Was this another test—and if so, what was it? *I am so close. Why now?*

He thought desperately. *The light is available to all. It is the space where I am. Step into light. And what then? And for that matter, how do I step into the light?*

Then he remembered what his father had said: "You have to move your life force."

Maybe if I put the two together, he wondered, *and I then have to step into the light? Well it's worth a try.*

He composed himself again. As he did so, he thought about the voice, his mother and father whom he loved so much, and his human friends. He reached out for the forest and felt its reassuring presence. The warm sun created patterns on the forest floor, the stillness so refreshing. Stillness. Silence. Space. Nothing. No thoughts. Quiet. Peaceful. Nothing. He felt so light. As if he didn't exist. Nothing, and yet part of everything. Warmth spread around him, a light growing brighter, beckoning, embracing, fulfilling.

Suddenly, light burst through him. Every cell in his body tingled with recognition, like an amazing memory surfacing from the depths of his mind with immense emotion.

"*Hello, Semaine,*" the voice said. "*Welcome to the light. Your journey's almost over, but you still have one final test.*"

Semaine timidly asked, "Why me?"

"*Why not you?*" said the voice. "*All living beings can quest for excellence in their own lives. There are no limitations to the good anyone can achieve. It's simply a choice to step into the light.*"

"Is this another riddle?"

"*Life can seem that way,*" answered the voice. "*It's not a complicated one, though. Like all things, it's in the quest, the journey, the adventure, that one can grow. The answers aren't always self-evident, and not always where one might think they are. And that is the real journey, the real experience that is available to all. Semaine, the light is where you will always find me. It is where you found me and where anyone can find me.*"

"*On your adventure, you were true to yourself, your family and your friends. You loved deeply, believed in yourself, and in times of great doubt and challenge, you were prepared to trust. To trust in me, a strange voice that sometimes came to you, and in yourself. Now it is time for you to return.*"

"I have so many other questions," said Semaine quietly.

"*There will be other times, Semaine. For now, remember always to look towards the highest good. In that direction, there are no limitations to what is possible.*"

The light faded. Semaine found himself once again alone with his thoughts, the forest, the stillness, and a deep sense of peace. With these feelings he once again reached out for all those he loved and as he did, he remembered his reason for being here. His quest was not quite finished yet. As the voice had said, he had one final test and so, in his heightened sense of awareness, he once again strove for his real self.

He again pictured his body, its texture, his tiny shaped claws, his curly tail, his tongue so adept at catching insects, and his shape. His concentration intensified; his visualisation strengthened and became more tangible. When he felt ready, he held the vision and allowed his own being to consume it, to become one with it, to become whole again. Slowly and surely, his life force became one with his projected self and once again he was overwhelmed with an emotional flood of imagery: bursting lights, as if a million stars from the heavens were exploding all at once—a rushing sensation, as if he were again travelling in the jeep, only a hundred times faster. The feelings merged and he had no time to think of anything except his projected image of himself. He sensed the very fabric of his skin, the texture of his tongue, the complex nature of his eyes. And still the world seemed to explode all around him.

Juanita and Semaine's father watched in amazement as the outline of a chameleon slowly took shape. It flickered and shifted, transparent, barely visible, and then it started to take shape, real, firm and then complete.

Semaine's chaotic transition slowly came to an end and he sat still on the branch. He let his senses reach out, finding his father, then Juanita, beside the log. He was filled with hope. Under his foot, he felt the log's roughness and he opened his eyes.

"Yes! I'm back!" He looked over at his father gleefully. "Good to see you, father."

"You too son." His father's voice was choked with emotion that his son was back… alive.

They crept towards each other and touched noses, cementing Semaine's return, expressing emotions that loved ones reuniting would recognise the world over.

Juanita watched the reunion, her own feelings of love already heightened by the Sacred Grove. Her relief that Semaine would live were also adding to her emotions. She felt tears on her cheeks as the two chameleons re-established their bond.

Semaine turned towards her and she lightly rested her palm on his back. Warmth spread through her hand and as it did, she heard Semaine's familiar voice.

"Juanita. Can you hear me?"

"Yes, Semaine. It's good to hear your voice. How does it feel to be yourself again?"

Semaine paused, reflecting for a moment on what had happened in the Sacred Grove, and he knew that telling some parts of this incredible adventure would wait for another time.

"Yes," he said, "It's good to be home. It's good to see my father again, and to see and feel my old self again. Juanita, I owe you all for your trust, your generosity, and your acceptance of me. I'm so glad I can still talk to you—and see my second family again before you go home."

Juanita lifted her hand and Semaine told his father what he was going to do. As Semaine turned back to the being, his father was still astounded by the communication between his son and the other being, even more so when the being reached out and touched his back in a gesture he sensed meant farewell. With Semaine nestling in her arms, Juanita walked slowly and carefully out of the Sacred Grove to where her family were waiting.

They greeted her with relief—she hadn't noticed how much time had passed, and Enrique was on the point of entering the Sacred Grove with the children to search for her.

They were overjoyed to see Semaine in his real form. Juanita put him on a log in the sunshine. Each family member had a last talk with Semaine and for each he had a message. For Maria, it was to follow her dreams. For Ramón, it was about having fun and continuing to be the best boy he could be. For Juanita and Enrique, it was about the difference they made to their family and community.

The family agreed to return often to the stump in the forest, where they could sit with Semaine and renew their unusual friendship. As Semaine watched them walk away, he felt sad, but honoured that he would see them again. He turned towards the grove, moving at his own pace at last, his adventure complete. It had been an amazing journey. Now it was time to share all his escapades with his father and mother.

Epilogue

It seemed so long ago, his adventure. The children were all grown up and had families of their own. Maria worked to preserve the forest as a natural habitat and was a respected advocate among her peers. Ramón studied animal behaviour, especially unusual family networks in the wild, and brought his research to society with the view that there was much humanity could learn from nature. Enrique was now the Alcalde of their small community and he and Juanita had a small, profitable business bringing technology and information to the town.

The family often visited Semaine as a group and sometimes individually, when they wanted to talk. He was now the chameleon community leader, had his own son and daughter, and was joined with the most wonderful chameleon lifemate, all of which was a whole other story.

As he sat on the log, the sun warming him with its life-giving force, he reflected once again on the cycle of life and how it fitted into a mysterious master plan. A master plan from which, he felt sure, the voice came. Yes, the voice still came, its messages always insightful and meaningful.

Semaine closed his eyes, felt again the sun's warmth, the refreshing breeze, and with the gentle memory of a family's laughter touching the corners of his mind and heart … he drifted off to sleep.

The End

Notes

Semaine is a work of fiction; however every effort has been made to create authenticity around the events in this book. For more information please access the following websites.

Andalucía - Protected natural environments in Andalucía. Nearly a fifth of Andalucía is protected, the largest proportion of an autonomous region in Spain, reflecting the unspoilt nature of its countryside and the high ecological importance of its territory.

For more information please go to:

www.andalucia.com

http://en.wikipedia.org/wiki/andalucia

Civil War - The Spanish Civil War was a major conflict fought in Spain from 17 July 1936 to 1 April 1939. An estimated total of 500,000 people lost their lives as a consequence of the War.

For more information please go to:

http://en.wikipedia.org/wiki/Spanish_Civil_War#cite_note-spanjudge-2

Common Chameleon - The Common Chameleon is the only species of Chamaleonidae of Europe. It is found in Southern Greece (Aegean Islands, Crete, Chios, Samos),Turkey (Aegean and Mediterranean cost) Malta, Southern Portugal, Southern Spain, Cyprus. In North Africa and the Middle East: Morocco, Algeria, Tunisia, Libya, Egypt, Israel, Palestine, Jordan, Western Sahara, Saudi Arabia, Yemen, Lebanon, Syria, Iraq, Iran.

For more information please go to:

http://en.wikipedia.org/wiki/Common_Chameleon
http://www.bbc.co.uk/nature/life/Chameleon

http://gis.wwfus.org/wildfinder/ (Go to this link, type *Chameleon* or *Chamaeleonidae* into the "search" bar on the world map.

Hurricanes – While rare, hurricanes and violent ocean storms occur off the coast of Spain and Portugal. For more information on hurricanes please go to:

http://www.nhc.noaa.gov/index.shtml (National Hurricane Centre)

http://en.wikipedia.org/wiki/Hurricane_Vince_(2005) and

http://www.hurriyet.com.tr/english/world/10851246.asp

Make a Difference

There are many charities protecting the habitats of different wildlife. Please take the opportunity to support non profit organisations that make a tangible difference across our world. An example of this is Rainforest Alliance. For more information please go to: www.rainforest-alliance.org

Semaine's Global Fundraising Campaign

To compliment World Environment Day (WED) an initiative of the United Nations Environment Programme (UNEP), we are proud to announce our charity of choice is the Rainforest Alliance. This global fundraising campaign is to help provide funds for multiple projects run by the Rainforest Alliance in over 70 countries across our world.

To donate funds directly to Semaine's Global Fundraising Campaign for Rainforest Alliance please go to: http://my.rainforest-alliance.org/goto/semaine